I0834305

The Carpenter's Maid

Contact Information: CastleRomanceNovels@Gmail.com

Table of Contents

Chapter 1 – The Hotel Hottie

I was thirty-six years old when I met Olivia. She was a chambermaid at the hotel I was staying at during the week. I build houses for a living, and my current home build was about three hours away from my house and I didn't feel like traveling back and forth every day. I had already sent my crew home to be with their families. I only had a few odds and ends to do in the house and then I was going to head back home myself. It was late January 2017, a bit chilly, and I had to go back to the hotel to grab something, and then I was going to eat some lunch before returning to the job site to finish up the house. It was right around twelve noon when I got back to the hotel.

I had noticed that there was a different lady cleaning my room; not the one I had gotten used to seeing every day. This new maid looked a lot younger, and I have to say, she was very attractive and very shy. She must have been in the middle of cleaning my room when I arrived, so it gave me the opportunity to talk with her briefly as she continued working. I wasn't blatantly hitting on her, so I'm sure she didn't feel nervous around me. She was changing the sheets on my bed, and I didn't mind her being in my room at all. In fact, it was my chance to get to know her a little bit, and sort of flirt with her. At first glance she looked Russian to me, and later I found out that I was right. Her English was not perfect, and she did have a very strong accent, which I found to be very sexy. She had longer than shoulder length blonde hair with dark highlights. She was about 5'6" tall and had a very toned, petite body. I really loved looking into her grayish blue eyes, they were very alluring. I didn't want to come across as overly aggressive, so I chose my words wisely. Honestly, I did have a very hard time taking my eyes off her. I'm sure she got hit on a lot. She looked a little upset. I could tell something was bothering her, but as a complete stranger, I doubted that she would tell me, so I didn’t ask.

Me: “You're doing a great job in my room young lady, and I just wanted you to know that. The room smells very nice. My name is Julian, by the way. And who might you be?”

Olivia: “Hi Julian, I am Olivia, and thanks for the compliment. Those are hard to come by around here. Everyone around here is so standoffish.”

Me: “How is your day so far? Has it been a productive day for you?”

Olivia: “Not bad. I got here late today, and my boss is a little upset with me. I keep getting the cold shoulder from her and it makes me uncomfortable. She doesn’t talk to me as it is, and she’s always trying to find mistakes in my cleaning. She makes me nervous. I don’t enjoy this anymore. I’m sorry, that’s too much information. I’m sure you don’t need to hear about my problems, I apologize. And quite honestly, I’m flattered that you’re even taking the time to talk with me. Thank you for that, Julian.”

Me: “How long have you been working here, Ms. Olivia?”

Olivia: “This is my third month, and I don't have a car. A friend of mine usually brings me back and forth to work, but I can't always count on her. So, I either have to call in to work, or walk almost three miles to get here, and I really don't like doing that, because when I get here, I'm already exhausted and want to go back home. I don’t mean to ramble on, please forgive me. I guess I’m just venting to you.”

Me: “Do you like cleaning rooms? Me personally, I hate cleaning up after people, especially if they’re inconsiderate slobs.”

Olivia: “I don't mind cleaning, but I would rather be cleaning my own house and not all these rooms every day. It gets boring very fast, and I don't enjoy it anymore after I'm in the third or fourth room. I try not to think about it too much, but it’s very hard not to.”

Me: “It sounds like being a chambermaid is not your life’s calling. Maybe this job isn't right for you."

Olivia: “Well, it's all that I could find right now. The pay is not that great either."

Me: “I'm sure it's hard to pick up after other people. I'm sure some of them can be real slobs.”

Olivia: “Oh yeah. I came across some filthy people. I’m just doing this until I can find something better. And it doesn't help much that I still don't have a car. I have been saving for one though.”

Me: “You feel trapped here, right?"

Olivia: “Yeah, it sort of feels like that. And to be honest, this is not for me. I just hope that this is a rut that I can work my way out of. Oh, well.”

Me: “I'm sorry you're not happy. But you never know, doors open and close all the time."

Olivia: “***Yeah?*** Well, ***this*** door hits me in the ass every day." She chuckled.

Me: “I'm willing to bet that once you close this door, another will open up immediately. Every face should have a smile on it, especially one as pretty as yours. I really want to see you smile, Ms. Olivia.”

Olivia: “You're very flattering, sir. You’re making me feel like I’m something special, which I am not.”

Me: “You don't have to call me sir. My name is Julian, and I may have an opportunity for you if you're interested."

Olivia: “Please don't tell me that you own a hotel." We laughed.

Me: “No, actually I'm in need of a maid for my house. It's a rather unique situation. Do you want to hear about it?"

Olivia: “Ok. I'm listening."

Me: “I'm a carpenter, I build houses. I've been out this way for several weeks now because the house I'm building right now is not far from here, and I didn’t want to drive three hours each way from my house. So, I chose this hotel, which, coincidentally, led me here to you.”

Olivia: “Do you build them to turn them over and sell them, or do you build them for other people?”

Me: “For other people. Well, first, before I tell you all about it, I don't want to take you away from what you're doing. How long do you usually have to clean this room?"

Olivia: “Usually, no more than an hour, but I’m at the point where I just don't care anymore. And besides, I'm just about due for my lunch break."

Me: “We can talk about it then. I don’t want to get you into any kind of trouble.”

Olivia: “No, keep going. I'll just stay here and take my break, if you don’t mind. I do need to step out and have a smoke really quick. My nerves are already shot.”

Me: “I’ll join you for a smoke if you’re ok with that.”

Olivia: “Yes, of course I am.”

I didn't know if she had brought lunch, or if she was hungry, so I offered to buy her something since I was going to have some food delivered to my room. She said she wasn't hungry but I'm going to order us lunch anyways.

Me: “Do you like pizza and wings?"

Olivia: “I ***love*** pizza and wings. Who doesn't?"

Me: “Good, then that's what we're having for lunch."

Olivia: “Well, if you insist, but don't feel like you have to do this for me."

Me: “Are you from around here, Ms. Olivia?”

Olivia: “Yeah, I grew up not too far from here, in a small farming community."

Me: “You're a country girl?"

Olivia: “I am, and somehow, I ended up ***here***. I want to be back out in the country, where I belong.”

Me: “I'm thirty- six years old, and how old are you, Ms. Olivia, if you don't mind me asking?"

Olivia: “Actually, today is my twenty- seventh birthday. I thought about calling in, but I need the money. I got here late today, and my boss just gives me an attitude and treats me like shit, as usual."

Me: “Did she at least wish you a happy birthday?"

Olivia: “No, I don't think she even knows, I'm sure no one knows. Why would they care anyways?”

Me: “Well happy birthday, young lady. I think you're done working for the day."

Olivia: “Yeah, I wish. That would be a great birthday present.”

Me: “Ok now, let me explain my situation to you. I live on my own in a rather big house out in the country. Now, I've been a bachelor for a very long time, and I really don’t have a knack for cleaning. I mean, I do keep my place clean, but cleaning bores the shit out of me. And to be honest, I’m not very fond of doing laundry and I don't have much interest in cooking.”

Olivia: “What do you do for food? Don't you ever go grocery shopping?"

Me: “I'll shop for groceries, but I only get the bare minimum. Now, here's my offer to you, Ms. Olivia. On the very front of my house is a separate apartment, sort of like an in-law’s type thing. It's attached to the house, and the only thing separating it from the main house is a sliding door. It has everything an apartment should have. I've never rented it out before, so I'm sure it's quite dusty and in need of a very thorough cleaning."

Olivia: “But I wouldn’t have any money to pay you rent, and I would need time to find a job.”

Me: “Well, there's a solution for that. If you come and stay at my house, and do the cleaning, laundry, and cooking, I'll pay you $300 a week in cash and you'll get the apartment as part of the deal, for free. So, you'll have your very own place, and spending money. And we'll work on getting you a car. Does that interest you at all?"

Olivia: “Why would you do that for me? You just met me and we’re complete strangers.”

Me: “We're not strangers anymore, and we're in a situation where we can help each other out. I leave nothing to chance, ever. I’d love to have you working for me instead of not being happy here at this shady hotel. It’s a lot to think about, and I know you’ve already had an overwhelming day. It saddens me to see you just so miserable being here, and you don’t have to waste any more time here.”

Olivia: “Are you pulling a birthday prank on me, Julian?" She laughed.

Me: “No prank, it's a legitimate offer. It helps ***me*** out and gets ***you*** away from here. What is your current living situation?"

Olivia: “I'm staying with a friend; the same friend that said she'd bring me back and forth to work. But she goes out to the bars every night and hardly ever comes home. So, then I don't have a way to get to work. When she does decide to come home, she brings home guys that she meets in the bars, and I have to listen to her get laid all night. She’s always trying to set me up with guys, but I just don’t want to be bothered by that. Julian, you don’t have to call me Ms. Olivia, just Olivia will be fine.”

Me: “You need more stability in your life, Olivia. What you’re telling me is far from stable."

Olivia: "I know it's not, but it's all I have right now. I shouldn't have left home when I did. I just wanted to explore life on my own for a little while to see if I could handle being independent. I was staying with an aunt before I got this job, but I felt like I was being a burden to her, and we didn't really get along too good. I felt it best to just leave, so I moved in with my so-called friend, and here I am."

Me: "What I'm offering you is a chance to start over. But it is about three hours from here, so you'd have to consider that. It's a lot to ask of you. I'll trust you blindly, and I hope you do the same for me. I swear, I'm not a stalker or creep, Olivia. An opportunity has presented itself to us."

Olivia: "When would you need me to start, if I did decide to take you up on your offer? I'm not someone who handles sudden changes very well, and it would probably scare the shit out of me, to be honest."

Me: "Today is Thursday, and I'll need to know by tomorrow, because that's when I'm heading back home. I have less than two hours' worth of work left in this house, but I was going to stay until tomorrow night. Or if need be, I could come back and get you at another time, if you're interested."

Olivia: "Take me with you. I'm ready to leave here."

Me: "Do you want the job? If you do, I'll pick you up tomorrow, and then we can head out, ok? I know it's on very short notice, but I do have to get home to prepare for another home build."

Olivia: "No, I mean take me with you, ***right now***. I'll go with you to finish up the house you're working on. I'm not afraid to get my hands dirty. Please, Julian, take me with you."

Me: "Are you being serious right now?"

Olivia: "Yes. I'll go. Get me out of here. I hate it. I'm willing to fly blind with you and take a chance."

Me: "I swear to you, Olivia, this is for real. I do realize that this sudden change of plans is going to scare you and make you nervous, but believe me when I tell you, I will take care of you, Olivia. We would have to swing by your current place and grab your clothes and personal effects. If there's any large furniture that you want to bring with you, we can come back and grab them at a later date."

Olivia: "I don't have any furniture to bring, but I do have a few personal and sentimental items that I cannot be without, especially my photo albums. There are some very precious pictures in them of my parents and childhood memories."

Me: "Ok, then that's what we're going to do. We'll leave right after we've had our lunch."

Olivia: "Is this really happening right now, Julian?"

Me: "Come with me for a minute, Olivia."

Olivia: "Where are we going?"

I took her by the hand and walked her down to the rental office. We walked in together and she was completely shocked at what happened next. She got very nervous and held my hand very tightly.

Rental Manager: "Can I help you, sir?"

Me: “Are you this young lady's boss?"

Rental Manager: “No, but I can get her for you. What does this pertain to?”

Me: “Good. Get her."

Olivia's boss walked out and asked her why she wasn’t in her rooms cleaning. And then her boss looked at me with a puzzled look on her face.

Her boss: “What’s going on here, sir? How can I help you?”

Me: “I just wanted to tell you that Olivia and I are checking out shortly.”

Her boss: “***Excuse me?*** Olivia is supposed to be in her rooms cleaning right now.”

Me: “We're leaving. She's done working for you, and I'm signing out of my room after her and I have had our lunch."

Olivia was so shocked by the situation that she just stared down at the floor. She got very nervous and grabbed my hand even tighter.

Her boss: “Olivia, you could have at least given me a little notice if you planned on leaving here.”

Me: “Umm, yeah, about ***that!*** She’s just showing you the same courtesy that you’ve always shown her.”

Her boss: “Well, if Olivia is leaving, then she has to leave that uniform here. She can't take it with her."

Me: “Fair enough. Olivia, you heard her, take the uniform off."

Olivia: “What? Here? ***Right now?*** You’re kidding, right?”

Me: “Yes, here, right now."

Olivia: “But I don't have any clothes to put back on. ***Are you being serious right now, Julian?*** “

Me: “Olivia, the uniform. Take it off please, so we can move on."

Olivia walked towards the employee break room, grabbed her jacket off the hook, clocked out, and then went into the bathroom to take off her uniform. When she walked back out to the lobby where I was, she threw her uniform towards her boss. All she had on were panties, a bra, and her jacket.

Olivia: “Can we please go before someone walks in? Please, Julian?”

Me: “Oh, we’re going. And we are never coming back here. Blow your ex-boss a nice kiss, Olivia, and say goodbye to her.”

Olivia: “You’re a very rude boss and I hope your whole staff quits on you.”

On the way back to my room I was walking a little bit behind her, trying to get a good look at her ultra-fine ass, which I did. Her jacket didn’t cover her ass, so of course I noticed that she had red panties on, which is my favorite color. I really loved how her ass cheeks wiggled when she walked.

Me: “Damn, Olivia, you have a very beautiful body. And I say that with complete respect."

Olivia: “Yeah? Do you like what you see? Well guess what? Me and this body are leaving with you. So, lead the way."

Our food arrived just as we made it back to my hotel room. Olivia was a basket case, but eventually calmed down enough to where we could have a civilized conversation. We both wanted to leave the hotel, so we collected my things, and then headed over to her place to grab her belongings. We were eating our food in my truck. Her roommate wasn't home, but Olivia did call her cell phone to tell her that she was moving out. Olivia got dressed and then put the rest of her clothes and personal effects in a garbage bag. Within ten minutes we were off to finish up that house I was building. It shouldn't take me very long to wrap things up, just a few loose ends. When we got there, I told Olivia to stay in the truck and keep it running so she could keep warm, and finish eating her lunch. Just over an hour later, I was all finished up, and we were off to my house. I was snacking on pizza and wings as I was driving. Olivia was smoking a cigarette and became extremely quiet.

Me: "What's wrong, Olivia? Everything's going to work out for you." She didn't answer.

Olivia: "Did that really happen? Am I in the middle of some twisted dream? ***What the fuck!*** "

Me: "I'm sure you're a bit confused and overwhelmed right now, and that's ok. A lot has happened to you today. The best part is less than three hours away."

Olivia: "I just left everything behind. Granted, I didn't have much to leave behind. But still, it hurts me. You're the first person in a very long time that's actually been nice to me. Thanks for saving me from my silent hell, Julian."

Me: "You've been through a lot already today. Try and take a nap, and I'll wake you when we get home. We'll be there before you know it."

After a three-hour drive, we finally got back to my place. Olivia was still sleeping, and I felt bad waking her up. I reached over and rubbed her forearm. She woke up, still half asleep. She looked around, then wiped her eyes. She looked around again from side to side, over and over. Finally, she realized that she was at a different place in the middle of nowhere with a man she has only known for a few hours.

Olivia: "Are we here? Is this it, Julian?"

Me: "Yeah, this is it, we're home. It'll take a few minutes to soak in, I'm sure. Do you see that big picture window on the front of the house?"

Olivia: "Yeah, I see it." She wiped her eyes again.

Me: "That's the living room window of your new apartment. Are you excited to check out your new pad?"

Olivia: "Ok, I'm ready for this."

Parked in the driveway, to give you a visual; straight ahead, and off to the right, is the house. Olivia's place is right there in front, facing the road. To the right of the house is a large yard about the size of a football field, maybe a little shorter. Straight ahead down the driveway is a huge deck that I built, attached to the left side of the house. And directly behind the deck, in the distance is a three-car garage that I also built several years ago. Off to the left of the driveway is another large yard, also about the size of a football field. The place is surrounded by very old, very large pine trees.

We walked into the house, and Olivia walked around a bit. She was actually impressed at how clean it was. It was far from being spotless, but still presentable. I'll give her the full tour later, but first I want her to see her new place. Her apartment butted up to the kitchen.

Me: "Hey, slide that door open and tell me what you see. Please excuse the dust and the mess. I haven't been inside here for quite a while. I hope it's to your liking."

She slid it open and there it was, her very own apartment. When you slide the door open you have to go down three steps into her place. She walked down the steps and looked around. She opened the cupboards, the curtains, and checked out the bathroom, which is quite big. The last door she opened was to her bedroom, which was to the left as you walk down the steps. There was a full-size bed in there with dressers. Everything was there for her. I noticed that she didn't bring a lot of clothes with her.

Me: "Is this going to do it for you? It's nothing fancy, but with a lady's touch, it could be."

Olivia: "I love it. I'm speechless. Are you sure you want to do this for me?"

Me: "I've already done it for you, so of course, I'm sure. It's a lot of area to keep clean, but I want you to know that I'm not expecting you to clean your ass off all day, every day. Just try to do the bare minimum. I don't care if you just work one day a week. I want you to feel at home here, so just slowly and gradually keep busy. I'm sure you'll know what and when to do something. Do you understand?"

Olivia: "I understand. Thank you so much. I don't know how I can ever repay you."

Me: "There will be no repaying in this house. You're helping me out as much as I'm helping you out. This is "*our*" place now, not just mine. You're the lady of the house, which reminds me, we have to get you some clothes, because I noticed that you didn't bring many with you. So, here's the deal; there is a small store down the road a bit. Tell me what your sizes are, and I'll zip down there really quick and grab you some clothes. Soon, we'll go shopping together and get you some really nice outfits. Sound good?"

Olivia: "That sounds good. Are you sure you don't want me to go with you?"

Me: "Of course I want you to go with me, but you've had an exhausting day, so just stay here and get a feel for the place. I won't be long. When I get back, we'll make something to eat."

Olivia: "I still have all that pizza in my belly, but thanks for offering."

She told me her pants and shirt sizes, and whatever else she might need to hold her over.

Me: "While I'm gone, walk around and take it all in and get acclimated. I'll grab a couple bottles of wine while I'm out. I'll be back soon."

Olivia: "Hurry back, please."

I bought her a couple of pairs of shorts, some pants, and a few shirts just to tie us over until we went shopping for better clothes. I remembered that it was her birthday today and I wanted to get her something nice, so I picked her up some perfume called "*Angel* ", some ice cream, bought a cake, and had the baker write her name on it. I wanted her to feel very secure here, especially since we've just recently become friends.

I got home from shopping, unloaded the truck, and headed into the house. Olivia was sitting at the table smoking a cigarette, and she had on one of my white T-shirts. I could clearly see she had taken off her bra. The bags with the cake, ice cream and her perfume were set off to the side.

Olivia: "I have to say that I'm really impressed with how clean this place is, considering you're a bachelor and you told me that you don't really like cleaning."

Me: "I do clean the house to keep it semi-presentable. Here's some clothes for you. See if they fit when you get a chance. And by the way, my shirt looks good on you. I should have bought you some of those."

Olivia: "I'll just wear yours in the meantime if that's ok."

Me: "What's mine, is yours. If my shirts fit you, you're welcome to wear them, anything you want."

She finished her smoke, and then grabbed the bag of clothes and brought them to her apartment. While she was in there, I took the cake out of the bag and set it on the table. It read "*Happy Birthday Olivia* ". This should make her day, and I hope it does; I'll find out shortly. I heard her walking back towards the dining room, so I sat at the table and waited for her. She saw the cake.

Olivia: "Julian? What's this?"

Me: "Well to me it looks like a cake for a special young lady named Olivia."

She took the moment in and started to cry. She then walked over to me and gave me a hug. I could hear her pouting, and I knew those were tears of happiness. She got her composure back and kissed me on the cheek.

Olivia: "I can't believe you did that. You remembered it was my birthday. This is the best day I've had in a very long time, all thanks to you. You're spoiling me, Julian. I don't deserve this."

Me: "Sure you do, Olivia. Welcome to your new life. I hope you'll find it very rewarding. Oh, and by the way, there's also ice cream in that bag, so we better get eating."

We had some cake and ice cream, and she made us some coffee. We went out and sat on the deck. I had a small table out there, and that's where we had our coffee.

Olivia: "Is that a hot tub? I've never been in one before. I hear they are very relaxing, and a great way to finish off a stressful day."

Me: "That is a hot tub, yes. I haven't used it in a while, so I have to give it a good cleaning before I fill it up. That's on my list of things to do. I'll have it cleaned in no time, and then we can both enjoy it together. Right about now that hot tub would feel great on my body."

Olivia: "I'll be right back. I have to use the ladies room."

While she was in the bathroom, I brought out the gift bag with her present in it. I forgot to mention that when I bought her the perfume, I also bought her a beautiful engraved white gold bracelet that read " *Worthy of Love* " on it. I couldn't wait to see her reaction. Hopefully once she saw her gifts, she'd forget about all her days of sadness. I heard her coming, so I got up and started looking out towards the trees, not paying attention to her, and acting like I didn't know there was a gift bag on the table for her. It had her name on it. She saw the bag and grabbed what was inside. I heard her flip open the box with the bracelet in it. She sniffled and started pouting quietly.

Olivia: "Can you come here for a minute please, Julian?"

Me: "Yeah, everything ok?"

She came towards me and grabbed me with a tight hug. She was so emotional that all I could do was hug her while rubbing her back. The crying came out and I just tried to comfort her the best I could.

Me: "It's ok, Olivia. You are worthy of happiness, and you are safe here, I promise."

Olivia: "I'm sorry. I just don't know how to react to all these beautiful gestures. This bracelet is beautiful. I'll never be able to thank you enough. I will never take it off."

She got so excited about the bracelet that she didn't notice that there was another gift in the bag.

Me: "I think there's one more thing in the bag. It's probably the receipt. Or is it just some wrapping paper, I can't tell."

She saw the perfume and immediately opened the box. She sprayed some on her forearm and smelled it. She was obviously familiar with the smell of it, and she smiled at me. She was smiling from ear to ear.

Olivia: “How did you possibly know that this is my favorite perfume?"

Me: “I didn't know. But I do remember a lady wearing that perfume, and I loved the way it smelled. So, I asked her what it was, and she told me.”

Olivia: “Are you deducting all of this from my first paycheck?" She chuckled.

She's had an emotional day so far. I'm glad she can start to feel joy and happiness. After sitting out on the deck for about two hours, we decided to order some Chinese food. She kept staring at her bracelet. It looked beautiful on her, and not to mention she had her perfume on, and damn, she smelled nice. I left to get the food and told Olivia to make herself at home, put on the TV, the radio, whatever she wanted. When I got back with the food, she had the TV on. She was watching some horror movie. She changed her mind about watching it and settled for a home cooking show. I bought a few more bottles of wine to have on hand.

Me: “Food is here. Let's dig in. You ***have*** to be hungry. I know I am."

Olivia: “I can definitely eat. I saved room for the Chinese food. I didn't know you played guitar."

Me: “Oh yes, it's my passion. I’ve been playing since I was twelve; self-taught."

Olivia: “Will you play for me sometime? I'd love to listen to you."

Me: “Of course I will. I'll even teach you how to play if you want to learn."

Olivia: "That's an interesting visual."

Me: "What is?"

Olivia: "Oh, nothing. I'm just pondering some thoughts."

My couch was one of those pullout sofas. I pulled out the mattress and asked her to come sit down and relax. We found a movie to watch, and we just sat there chilling, talking, and eating. There wasn't much that we didn't talk about. She was very easy to talk to, and I don't think she felt uncomfortable at any time. It was very hard for me to keep my eyes off of her. I'll admit, I was instantly attracted to her the moment I laid eyes on her at the hotel. I really do love looking into her beautiful eyes; they're very mesmerizing. Olivia is a very sexy and beautiful young lady. She has the most beautiful blonde hair.

Me: "So, did you have a good birthday? Was it a good day?"

Olivia: "It was a great day once I got here. I'm still wrapping my head around all that has happened today, and how everything was completely unplanned and spur of the moment. A lot has happened so fast for me. For you as well, I'm sure."

Me: "Well, sometimes in life it's healthy to do things spontaneously. If you did everything "*normal*" then life would be boring. At least I think so. I tend to go against the grain a lot. Dare to be different, girl. You can do whatever you want here and be whoever you want, I will never judge you."

Olivia: "Are you spiritual at all, or religious?"

Me: "I'm definitely not religious, but I am very spiritual, a free thinker. Are you?"

Olivia: "I don't know if there's a God, but I do think there is a heaven. I believe in angels and guardians. And when I stare off into space, I have to wonder if there are other beings out there. There's too many planets and stars for us to be the only living things."

Me: "I agree with you one hundred percent. From what I make of the human race so far, there are a lot of dumb ass fucks walking this earth." She chuckled.

Olivia: "You're funny, so easy to talk with. You have completely brightened up my day, you have no idea, Julian. Where have you been all my life? I needed to meet you a long time ago."

It was getting late, and we both had a long, eventful day. We got done with our food and she said she wanted to get some rest. She kept touching and spinning her bracelet around her wrist. I'm glad she liked it. She looked me dead in the eyes and told me to close mine. I did, and she leaned over and gave me a quick kiss on the lips.

Olivia: "It was a very special day for me. The bracelet is stunning. I absolutely adore it. I'm going to have one more smoke and then call it a night. I'll start cleaning tomorrow morning."

Me: "I want you to relax for the rest of the week, ok? You have plenty of time to clean, don't be in a hurry. Let's just spend the next few days getting to know each other better."

Olivia: "Ok, good night, Julian. I will see you in the morning. Thanks again for a very beautiful day and thank you for the most beautiful birthday I've had in a very long time."

She had her smoke, and then headed into her apartment. I could hear her moving things around, and then eventually I heard nothing. She must have gone to bed. I was exhausted but couldn't sleep yet. I laid there in silence reflecting on the day and hoping that tomorrow would be just as good. While she was sitting next to me on the couch, she was wrapped up in a little fleece blanket that I had on the back of the couch. I spent a few minutes looking at it in the exact spot where she was sitting. I reached over, grabbed it, and smelled it. It smelled just like the perfume I had bought her. That, to me, was sexy.

I fell asleep on the sofa bed and woke up around 7:00 a.m. the next morning. Olivia was already up having her coffee and a smoke at the table. She got up and poured me a cup of coffee, lit me up a smoke, and handed it to me. She was definitely not shy about showing off her amazing body in front of me. It must mean that she's comfortable being here with me. I do believe that she already trusts me to some degree.

Olivia: "Good morning, handsome man. Did you sleep well last night?"

Me: "Yes, I did. And how did you sleep?"

Olivia: "I slept great once I was ***able*** to fall asleep. I kept thinking of how beautiful yesterday was, and how everything happened so fast and unplanned. Thank you for such a beautiful birthday, Julian. It meant a lot to me, it really did."

Me: "I'm glad you enjoyed it, Olivia. I'm also glad you chose to come here to be in this house with me."

Olivia: "I'm still a little scared by the whole thing, you know. I'm experiencing new feelings, and I hope I can understand them as I feel them."

Me: "You'll be fine, young lady. You'll learn to trust me fully and know that I mean you no harm. I want you to feel safe here. The world outside these walls can be very unforgiving."

Olivia: "I do trust you, Julian, and you make me feel very safe and secure here. I love being out in the country, away from all the noises of the towns and cities. The air out here is so pure and refreshing. Do you have to work today?"

Me: "No. I'm starting a new home build on Monday. So, I get to relax all weekend with my White Russians and Bloody Mary's."

Olivia: "That's funny, because I'm Russian. My parents are Russian immigrants."

Me: "I had a feeling that you were Russian. I knew it the moment I looked into your eyes. I like my Bloody Mary's in the morning and my White Russians in the evening."

Olivia: "Well then, my first task of the day is making you your Bloody Mary. Are you at least going to wait until I've made you some breakfast first?" She chuckled.

Me: "I suppose I can wait if I absolutely have to."

We finished our coffee, and then went outside on the deck for some fresh air. It wasn't too cold out, and the sun was out, not a cloud in the sky. She did put on one of my sweatshirts to keep a little warmer. She also wore tight leggings and those long, thick socks that go up to your knees. I don't know what they're called.

Olivia: "If I dress a little too provocative around you, please let me know, Julian. I'm stuck in the habit of wearing next to nothing when I'm home."

Me: "Olivia, dress however you want. I told you before, I will never judge you. You have an amazing body and there's nothing wrong with showing it off."

Olivia: "Thank you for understanding me."

Me: "Olivia, you are a very sexy and beautiful young lady. I'll try my best to keep my eyes off you."

Olivia: "What if I don't want you to?" She winks.

Chapter 2 – Getting Acclimated

It was February now, Valentine's Day, actually. When Olivia came out of her apartment this morning, there were a dozen white roses on the dining room table, along with a card and some chocolates.

Olivia: "Julian, what did you do? These roses are so beautiful. How did you know that I preferred white roses over the red?" She smells them.

Me: "Well, I didn't have a date for Valentine's Day, so I figured we could spend it together, unless you have other plans. And as far as the white roses, well, I think they're nicer to look at than the red, so I took a chance."

Olivia: "Oh Julian, I would love to spend it with you. The card is beautiful, thank you so much. I hope that I'm the only woman that you bought roses for. So, am I the only one?"

Me: "Honestly? There is one other woman besides you, and I hope that you're not feeling slighted by that. She's someone that I've known and loved for a very long time. I'm just being honest with you."

Olivia looked at me as though her heart had sunk to her feet.

Olivia: "I understand. Really, I do. You're a very handsome man and I'm sure you've always had women coming around here to see you. Just please promise me one thing."

Me: “Sure, anything, Olivia.”

Olivia: “If you decide to invite another woman here, please let me know ahead of time so I could make myself scarce. That may rub me the wrong way. And I’m being honest with ***you*** right now.”

Me: “Olivia, the other woman I’m referring to is my mother. I always send her roses on Valentine’s Day. I have no other intimate interest besides you.”

Olivia: “Why did you get me going like that? That wasn’t funny...***honey***.”

Me: “I’m sorry, Olivia, for the way I dragged that out. Do you forgive me? Please?”

Olivia: “Of course I forgive you, smart ass. Please don’t do that again.”

She sniffled a little, came up to me, and kissed me on the cheek as we hugged.

Me: “I wanted you to have a special Valentine’s Day, and I’m so glad you’re here to share it with me. I really love having you here.”

Olivia: “Julian, you have already touched my life in so many beautiful ways. You have no idea. The past three weeks of my life have been so amazing.”

Me: “Well, to be honest with you, your being here makes this house such a better place to live in.”

Olivia: “When are you going to be working close to home, so you can come here for lunch every day?"

Me: “Actually, there's a house I'm building right up over the hill. You could see it from here if you were to stand on the roof. I’ve been bouncing back and forth between that one and other jobs. So, after next week I'll be working there for quite a while.”

Olivia: “That will be awesome, having you close to home. I’m sure you’re excited about that.”

Me: “Yeah. Within two weeks or so I'll have all my other projects wrapped up so I can focus on this huge build. I'm looking forward to it. I’m also looking forward to coming home for lunch. What a luxury that will be. Of course, it doesn’t hurt that you’re here either.” She winked at me.

Olivia: “You’re very flattering. You really know how to put a smile on my face. Do you have to work today, or do I get you all to myself?”

Me: “I do have to take a ride over to the job site to drop off some blueprints for my guys. Would you like to come along? I’ll only be there for a little bit.”

Olivia: “I don’t want to impose.”

Me: “You won’t be imposing, Olivia, not at all. Come with me, and then we could go out for lunch. How does that sound?”

It was around 10:00 a.m. when Olivia and I headed over to the job site. Once we got there, Olivia waited in my truck. My guys were wondering who the hot blonde was in my truck, so I motioned for Olivia to come over to where we were. I’m sure as with all or most guys, they were checking her out as she was walking towards us. My right-hand man, Eric, was the first to make a comment.

Eric: "Bro, she's fucking hot. Where did you meet her? ***Damn!*** "

Me: "She was one of the maids at the last hotel we stayed at while we were doing that huge addition on the back of that waterfront property."

Olivia was getting closer to us, so the conversation about her stopped.

Olivia: "Good morning, guys."

Me: "Guys, this is Olivia. Olivia, these are my friends/co-workers; Eric, Mike, Greg, and Dave."

They all said hello to Olivia with their tongues practically hanging out of their mouths.

Olivia: "Julian speaks very highly of his crew. He says you guys are the best around."

Eric: "Well, we're definitely no slouches, and we owe it all to Julian. He's a very good teacher and the best boss anyone could ever hope for."

Mike: "Julian said that you're a maid at the hotel we all stayed at last month. I don't remember seeing you there, but obviously Julian did. It's a pleasure to meet you."

Olivia: "Well, that's partially true. I ***was*** a chambermaid there while you guys were there, but I've changed jobs since then."

Dave: "What do you do now, if you don't mind me asking?"

Olivia looked over at me, not sure of how she should answer Dave's question.

Me: "You can tell them, Olivia."

Olivia: "I live with Julian now, in his spare apartment. I'm ***his*** maid now, and I love it."

Greg: "Holy shit, Julian. When did that happen?"

Olivia: "If memory serves me correctly, it was his last day at the hotel. That was the day that I met him, and that was also the day that I left with him."

Eric: "You have a very strong accent. What nationality are you?"

Olivia: "I am Russian."

Dave: "Julian, you're an animal, bro." Olivia blushed.

Me: "Ok, let's not get into my personal life, guys. We have plenty of time to chit chat about it. I just wanted to drop off these blueprints."

Olivia: "Maybe Julian will buy me my very own tool belt and teach me the trade as well."

Mike: "Yeah, I could picture that." We all laughed.

Me: "Ok guys, I have to go. The roof rafters are supposed to be here around 1:00 p.m. as long as they're not running behind. Just make sure they set them where they're supposed to be, and then you guys can call it a day. I will see you tomorrow."

After Olivia and I left the job site, we decided to go grab a bite to eat at the local diner. She was wearing the perfume that I bought her for her birthday. She has yet to take off the bracelet that she got from me. I noticed that she didn't have her own cell phone, so after our lunch that's where we were going next, but she didn't know that yet.

Me: "The food here is exceptionally good. I come here all the time."

Olivia: "You must meet a lot of people in your profession. Yes?"

Me: "I sure do. I've met a lot of great people. In my line of work, it's very important to spread the word around, hoping to land new jobs."

Olivia: "Can I ask you something, Julian?"

Me: "Of course you can. Please don't ever hesitate to ask me anything."

Olivia: "I'm sure that your employees are going to have a lot of questions for you concerning me. And I guess I'm just curious what your response is going to be if they ever ask you just how involved we are. I mean, I'm sure that right about now they're all talking about the blonde that you brought to the job site. So, are you going to tell them that we are just friends, or more than just friends?"

Me: "I will tell them that the moment I laid my eyes on you, there was no way on this earth that I was going to let you slip away. With me is where I wanted you to be."

Olivia: "I understand that part of it, but do you really have an interest in being more than friends, or do you want to keep it strictly platonic?"

Me: "Olivia, I have yet to make a pass at you. I certainly don't want to overstep my bounds with you, and I'm trying to earn your trust. But in all honesty, I'm fucking crazy about you, and it's very hard being around you and not being able to just grab you and kiss you. Kissing is my favorite aphrodisiac."

Olivia: "So, you're hoping to be more than just friends? And I don't mean *"friends with benefits"*. I'm talking about an exclusive relationship. Is that what you're wanting?"

Me: "Yes, I want an exclusive, very serious relationship with you. But I'm afraid to make an effort to kiss you, not knowing how you really feel about me, and what you're really wanting to happen between us."

Olivia: "Julian, I would have ***never*** left the hotel with you if I wasn't interested in becoming more than friends with you. Two strangers meet, and the very day that they meet, they end up living together before the night is over. I mean, how often does that happen? ***Who does that?*** Obviously, that's what happened with us. I have absolutely no regrets. Do you?"

Me: "The only regret I have is not meeting you a long time ago." She smiled and blushed.

After we finished our meals, I told her that we were going to get her a cell phone. I have a land line in the house, I use it for my business, but I do want her to have her own phone. When we got in my truck, she lit up a smoke, handed it to me, and then lit one for herself.

Olivia: "Julian, I'm pretty sure that I don't have enough credit to get my own cell phone plan."

Me: "It doesn't matter because I'm adding you to my plan."

Olivia: "Honey...no. You've already done so much for me. Please don't."

Me: "Olivia, I want to do this for you."

So, that's what we did. She now had her very own cell phone. I'm not a wizard with smart phones but I did show her enough to navigate it. After she spent some time with it, she was more efficient at it than I was on mine. I would say that Olivia had a very nice Valentine's Day, as did I. I was chilling on the pullout sofa watching a movie when she decided to join me. She brought with her a bottle of wine and two glasses. She really dresses down when she's relaxing for the night. She was wearing super thin shorts and a T-shirt. I could tell that she didn't have a bra on because her nipples were protruding through the shirt. And as always, she was wearing that sexy perfume. We were both sitting up against the back of the sofa as we were drinking our wine and having a smoke. As we watched the movie, we shared some more of our favorite childhood memories. She lived a very reclusive life, just like I did. We also learned that we were both extreme introverts. She doesn't like sports and neither do I, but we both love music. She already knew that about me from seeing all the guitars and amplifiers in my music room.

Olivia: "So, I have a question for you. Are we considered boyfriend and girlfriend now?"

Me: "I would love to be your man, Olivia. Would you like to be my lady? For real? Exclusively?"

Olivia: "I thought you would never ask. Yes, I would love to be your lady, but only if you can promise me that none of your ex-girlfriends are going to be showing up at your door, wanting you back."

Me: "I promise you, Olivia, there is no one else in my life. It's just you and me, and this house. I trust that you will believe me when I say that."

It was at this time that we had our very first kiss, and it lasted for about five minutes. It was a very intense kiss, open lips, and tongues. We started to get carried away and started feeling each other's bodies. She didn't feel below my belt, although a few times she did move her hand over my crotch. I cautiously moved my hand over her breasts several times, but I wasn't trying to get her super horny. I already had a full erection, and she could clearly see it through my shorts.

Olivia: "You don't wear any underwear, do you?"

Me: "Umm...nope."

Olivia: "Well, that would explain why I've never seen any in our laundry basket. Of course, if you ***did*** wear underwear, I don't think it would have any effect on the way your cock is bulging through your shorts right now, not that I'm trying to notice."

Me: "I'm sorry, I should have told you. A good kiss will get me very hard, very fast. I love to kiss."

Olivia cleared her throat a few times as she kept looking into my eyes and at the bulge in my shorts. Her eyes were going back and forth.

Olivia: "Now that we're officially exclusive to each other, I have to tell you something, and I'm very afraid of your response. But I do need to tell you."

Me: "Olivia, please don't ever feel that you can't tell me something. You are my partner now and you can confide in me about everything."

She lit up a smoke, took a large gulp of her wine, and became silent for a few minutes, just staring off into space.

Olivia: "Julian, I'm a virgin. Does that change things between us?"

Me: "No, babe. I told you before, I will never judge you. Actually, that's pretty fucking hot."

Olivia: "Are you sure? Because the last guy I told that to literally got up and walked out the door, never to be heard from again."

Me: "Well, that guy's a fucking idiot, and if I ever see him, I will tell him that to his face. What? He couldn't get a piece of ass from you, so he bailed?"

Olivia: "Yes, to put it bluntly. Please understand that he was the only guy I've ever been with, and a kiss was as far as I went with him. It was a terrible kiss at that. He started getting very irritated with me because I kept pulling his hand away from my crotch area."

Me: "Olivia, you'll never have to worry about that with me. I happen to think that you're the best thing to ever walk into my life. I'll never forgive myself if I ever mess this up."

Olivia: "I kept telling myself all these years that I was going to be deeply in love with the man that takes my virginity. I do have old fashioned values, standards, and morals. I am sure that you've never had a problem getting women, so if I'm not exactly what you're looking for, I will completely understand. I can just be your maid and leave it at that."

Me: "Olivia, it took thirty-six years to find you. You were the lady in my dreams that I just couldn't get close enough to touch.

The more I dreamt about you, the closer I got to touching you, but you were still so far away. So, if you think that I'm going to let you go now, you're one hundred percent wrong. I think I'm falling in love with you. In fact, I'm ***sure*** that I am."

Olivia: "Do you really mean that? Please be sure of how you feel because I am falling deeply in love with you, and it would crush me to lose you now. There, I've said it."

That was a conversation that neither one of us expected to have, at least not for a while yet. I think we were both relieved that our true feelings came out, and neither of us felt any kind of rejection. We spent a little more time kissing before calling it a night. She went into her apartment, and I slept on the pullout sofa. I thought about her all night until I finally dozed off.

The following morning when I got up for work, Olivia was already sitting at the table having a smoke and a cup of coffee. She looked very beautiful rolling out of bed. Her hair was up in a bun, and she was wearing a short, silk mini robe that barely covered her ass. I went up to her, gave her a good morning kiss, grabbed a cup of coffee, and joined her at the table. She lit up a smoke and then handed it to me. Coffee and cigarettes go so good together, at least we think so.

Olivia: "Good morning sexy man. Did you sleep well?"

Me: "I did, yes. I fell asleep in love with the most amazing lady I have ever met. And how did you sleep, sexy lady?" She had the cutest blush.

Olivia: "Oh, honey, you always know what to say to me to put a smile on my face. What a beautiful way to start the day. I already have your lunch packed, sweetheart. I can't wait until you get to come home for lunch every day."

Me: "Have you called your parents at all to tell them that you've moved here with me?"

Olivia: "I have, honey. I haven't told them that we were together though. I think I'll wait for that. They're from the old country, and if they knew that I moved in with a man after just one day of knowing him, they're liable to think that their daughter is bat-shit-crazy." She chuckled.

Me: "It will probably be a long workday for me today. I have to finish up on this current build so I can start another one tomorrow. You have my number if you need anything. You can call me anytime you want. Just know that you will be on my mind, and I can't wait to come home to you."

I grabbed my lunch and a cup of coffee to go. While I was standing by the door, she grabbed me and gave me the most amazing kiss.

Olivia: "I love you, Julian. Please hurry home to me."

Me: "I love you too, babe. You are devastatingly gorgeous. See you soon."

While I was at work, Olivia put on the cooking channel and kept herself busy tidying up the house. She had the place looking amazing and it smelled so nice. She is a phenomenal cleaner; very thorough. She doesn't miss cleaning hotel rooms. She loves being here and is always in a great mood, especially now that she knows that I'm in love with her. I actually find it very sexy that she is still a virgin at twenty-seven years old. That's very uncommon these days.

My crew also noticed that since I've been with Olivia, I'm in a lot better mood. They all have wives to come home to so I'm sure they can relate to how I've been feeling. It makes for a better workday, but I miss Olivia so much when I'm not with her. I stopped wearing my watch because I found myself always looking at it, counting the minutes until I was on my way home to see my precious lady. Anyone who has been in love before will know exactly what I'm talking about.

Eric: "Hey bro, when's the wedding?"

Me: "Wedding? What wedding? Who's getting married?"

Mike: "Yours and Olivia's wedding. You are smitten for that girl. We can all tell, dude."

Me: "I don't know what you're talking about." I winked at them.

Dave: "If ***my*** wife looked like Olivia, I'd stop cheating on her." We all laughed.

Me: "Are you having an affair with someone that we don't know about?"

Dave: "Of course not. I'm just being silly. You know me."

Greg: "Does she speak Russian to you."

Me: "No. Not to me directly. But when she talks with her parents on the phone, all she speaks is Russian. To be honest with you, I really love her accent, it's sexy. I could listen to her talk for hours."

Olivia had a taste for sexy clothing, and when we bought her a new wardrobe, she asked me if there was a place that sold work outfits, like a nurse outfit or airline stewardess outfit, that sort of thing. I said that there was, and she asked if I would bring her to check out some outfits, so I did. When we got there, she told me to wait in the truck, she'd only be a minute. She ran in quickly and was back out in less than fifteen minutes. She came out with a big bag, so she must have bought something.

Me: “Did you see anything you liked?"

Olivia: “Not really, but they did have some rather nice throw blankets, so I picked up a few."

She hopped back in the truck, and we headed home. She was quite the cook and really enjoyed it. I was never going to starve, that's for sure. She wasn't one of those women who wore a lot of make-up. In fact, I don't think she wore any, except maybe some eye liner. She didn't need make up, she had natural beauty. She was the lady of the house and carried that title proudly. A lot of times when she was cooking or cleaning, she would shake her ass as she was listening to the music playing in the background. I really loved watching her move that body to the music. She was quite a dancer.

The next day when I got home from work, I walked in, but didn't see her. She usually saw me pulling up the driveway and met me at the door. She came out of her apartment in this very hot and sexy maid's outfit. That explained the sound of high heels I was hearing. She had her hair pulled back behind her ears. She looked absolutely stunning.

Olivia: “Welcome home, honey. Did you have a good day at work?"

Me: “Umm, yeah. ***Look at you! Holy shit, that’s sexy!*** “

Olivia: “You like it? I bought it the day we went to the outfit store."

Me: "You told me that you didn't see anything in there that you liked."

Olivia: "I know I said that. But there were also a few things in there that I absolutely ***loved***. So, I had to have them. Do I look ok? Is it too much?"

Me: "***Fuck no, it's not too much!*** You look stunning, Olivia. You are a very nice addition to this household."

Olivia: "Well, you did tell me to wear whatever makes me feel comfortable. And since I'm your maid, I may as well look the part."

Me: "I'm pretty sure that any working maid out there is not wearing anything as sexy as that, with the exception of maybe an escort."

Olivia: "Well, I hope you don't get too distracted by this. I wouldn't want you to lose your train of thought." She winks.

Me: "You are ***really*** enjoying this right now, aren't you? Am I supposed to look at you strut around in that outfit and not want to take you to bed?"

Olivia: "I just want to look good for you, honey. I want to feel sexy, look sexy, and smell sexy. I want you to look at me and crave me."

Me: "Of course I'm craving you. How could I not."

Olivia: "That's all I wanted to know. Dinner is almost ready. Make sure you save room for dessert."

She headed out to the kitchen, up to the stove and stirred the sauce very slowly. I quietly walked up behind her and got so close to her that my body was touching hers. I slowly started grinding up against her ass. She stopped stirring the sauce and kept looking straight ahead. I reached around her with my right arm and put my hand right between her legs. She kept looking straight ahead. I could hear her very quietly taking deep breaths. She started to moan softly. She turned around and looked me in the eyes for about five seconds.

Olivia: "Give me those lips, sweetheart. You're such an amazing kisser. It sends chills down my spine."

Me: "I've never kissed any lips that are as soft as yours. You too, are an amazing kisser."

Olivia: "Dinner is just about ready, baby, if you want to have a seat."

She made homemade sauce and rigatoni, a favorite of mine. She also whipped up a salad. She had the table dressed up very nice, as she usually did. We always sat across from each other. I got to look into those deep grayish blue eyes of hers. I got lost just looking into them. As I was talking and looking at her, she would periodically lick her lips, but only if she knew that I was looking at her.

Olivia: "Will you take me to work with you sometime so I can watch you build things?"

Me: "I sure will, babe. We'll wait until the weather starts getting warm again. How does that sound? I will even put you to work."

Olivia: "I don't mind hard work, sweetheart. I would love to learn more about your trade. We're building this relationship together, so I don't see why we can't build walls together." She smiled.

Me: "I will teach you the trade, honey. As a matter of fact, that house up over the hill is where I'm definitely going to need your expertise. I'm building it fully furnished, so all the owners have to do is basically move in. Everything will already be there for them."

Olivia: "Do you already have buyers for it?"

Me: "Yes, so it has to look stunning in every way possible."

Olivia: "How much is that house going to be worth when it's all done, if you don't mind me asking. I'm not trying to pry, sweetheart. I just have an interest in your profession, because I fully support what you do for a living, and I am certainly proud of you."

Me: "The house will be worth at least a half a million dollars, maybe more. That's on the conservative side. With the addition of the inground pool, probably a hundred thousand more."

Olivia: "It must be nice to have that kind of money laying around to buy a house that expensive. I can't wait to see it when it's done."

Me: "Starting next week, me and my crew will be working there until it's done."

Olivia: "Really, baby? You'll just be working up over the hill? It's going to be so nice having you here for lunch every day. I can even bring you and your crew some homemade chili for lunch."

Me: "We would love that a lot. I love homemade chili and

chicken noodle soup."

Olivia: "That's going to be awesome, a lunch date with my sexy man. I can't wait."

We had our after-dinner smoke and some wine. We decided to take a walk down the country roads and get some fresh air. It was a little brisk out, but we didn't care. Just the thought of us being together, holding hands was enough to keep us warm. I had a little bottle of whiskey in my pocket if we needed to take a few chugs to keep warm. Where we lived, it hardly ever snowed, and the temperature hardly ever gets below freezing. I showed her some of the older farmhouses in the area. We both loved being outside in the elements. Returning home from our walk, we took a shower together. Nothing happened in the shower other than kissing. We both kept our hands to ourselves, as hard as it was. After our shower, we had one more smoke, kissed good night, and headed to bed. She went into her apartment, and I crashed on the sofa while watching a movie.

Fast forwarding several weeks, we were well into the month of April now. Me and my guys have been working on that huge house up over the hill from my house. Me and Eric were there every day, but I did send Greg, Mike, and Dave off to do some smaller jobs, mainly home additions. I really loved working this close to my home, as did Olivia. It is a real treat coming home for lunch every day. Olivia made homemade chili, so I was excited about that. She also made homemade bread. Olivia loved to cook and was very good at it. Some days she would just bring my lunch to the job site so she could eat with Eric and me. She always made enough food for all three of us. It saved Eric from driving home for lunch.

The masons have been laying white Italian block around the

whole house and were very close to being done. The exterior of the house was just about wrapped up, so it was time to focus on interior designs.

We both decided to make a cup of hot chocolate and go sit on the two- person swing out on the deck. It wasn't quite dark out yet so we could see the deer out by the tree line. I love animals and am always feeding them around the house. The deer were there waiting for their apples so they could bed down for the night with full bellies.

Olivia: "Oh, honey, look at the deer out there. They are such beautiful animals. Please tell me that you don't hunt them."

Me: "I would never hunt deer, babe. I'm too much of an animal lover. Do you want to help me feed them their apples?"

Olivia: "I would love to."

I grabbed the bushel of apples off the porch, and we walked over towards the tree line. I usually cut the apples in quarters for them. Olivia was a little scared to get close to them, understandably so. Deer can be very intimidating up close, and if you provoke them, they could do some damage to you if you corner them. We got to within twenty feet of them and started throwing the apples towards them.

Me: "Look at the baby, honey. Aren't they adorable?"

Olivia: "Aww, honey, they make the cutest sounds. Can we have one for a pet?"

Me: "Trust me, babe, as long as we keep feeding them, they'll come around every night for us."

Olivia: "They know they're safe here with us. Yes?"

Me: "They sure do. I also feed the squirrels, birds, and bunnies."

It was getting late, so Olivia and I kissed good night and headed to bed. As always, she went to sleep in her bed, and I just chilled on the sofa trying to wind down. I could hear thunder way off in the distance. We always get a lot of rain and thunderstorms in April around here. Soon after that, I could hear it starting to rain. It started out lightly but picked up rather quickly.

I don't remember what time it was, but the thunder got very loud; loud enough to shake the windows. It woke me from a sound sleep. The next thing I remember was Olivia bolting out of her apartment and heading towards the couch. At first, she was going towards my bedroom, but she saw me lying on the sofa. She quickly laid down next to me and latched on to me tightly. She buried her head in my chest.

Olivia: "I hate the thunder when it gets this loud. It felt like my room was going to explode. And with the lightning flashing like that, it scares the shit out of me."

Me: "It's ok. You're safe. I got you."

Olivia: "Oh honey, when is it going to stop?"

She finally started calming down after about a half hour of me holding her. There we were, just holding each other, listening to the heavy rain and thunder. I didn't mind it too much, but my sweet Olivia was petrified. After a while, she fell asleep in my arms. The scent of her body was driving me crazy. I kept rubbing her back lightly and eventually, I fell asleep. It had to be an hour or so later when she turned and slept on her side, facing away from me. I'm a side sleeper so I turned also, and we were doing what a lot of people call "*spooning*". That is how we fell asleep that night, on the pullout sofa, holding each other.

Chapter 3 – The Consummation

It was now the month of June, and things were great between me and Olivia. She's a phenomenal cook, cleaner, and a beautiful human being. I adore her and it is a pleasure to have her here with me. When I first approached her about working for me and living here, I pondered the thought of her being more than just my maid. In the back of my mind, that's what I really wanted to happen. I mean, she is downright gorgeous and sexy. She has a dynamic personality, and she is such a warm and caring person. I can't say enough about her. She is exactly the kind of lady that I could spend the rest of my life with. I have never been with anyone who could even remotely compare to her.

I think at this point, without coming out and saying it, we were both wanting to make love. And what's going to make that so special is, when we finally do that, it will consummate this relationship and bring it to the level that it was meant to be at. It has been very hard seeing her here every day and not wanting to have sex with her. I'm sure that I'm speaking for her as well. That's why I love this relationship. That's why I have so much respect for her, and that's why I'm so in love with her.

Olivia: "Honey, can I ask you something?"

Me: "Of course you can, baby. Anytime that you have something on your mind that you need to share, please don't ever be afraid to speak up. You should know that by now, honey. I want you to confide in me about everything."

Olivia: "I've been living here for almost six months, and every night when we go to sleep, I sleep in my bed, and you have always slept on the fold out couch. I mean, I've never seen you come out of your bedroom in the morning. You have always slept on the couch. How come, baby?"

Me: "I don't think there's any real reason in particular. I'm so used to laying on the couch at night when I get home from work, that I just usually fall asleep on it, even before you ever came to live here."

Olivia: "But you have such a beautiful big bedroom. The bed is huge, and the view outside from the windows is beautiful and breath-taking."

Me: "That bed is definitely huge, It's a California King. I should start sleeping in it, huh?"

Olivia: "I would if that was ***my*** bed. It's so beautiful. I'll trade you."

Me: "That might be too much bed for your bedroom. You'd always be hitting it when you walked by it and start swearing like I do." She chuckled.

Olivia: "Well, I put fresh sheets on it, as well as pillowcases, in case you ever want to use it."

Me: "Thanks, babe. Hey, do you like fireworks?"

Olivia: "I ***love*** watching fireworks. Why? Did you buy some?"

Me: "No, but every year, the town has a huge display of them on the lake. I figured for the 4th of July we could have dinner on the lake before they start shooting them off. I know of a very secluded spot where we could lay a blanket down and sip some wine while watching the fireworks."

Olivia: "I would love that. I don't care what we do, sweetheart, as long as I'm with you. I just want to walk hand in hand with my guy and show the world how happy and in love we are."

Me: "Yes. Being in love is such an incredible feeling. I've never experienced it until I met you."

The next morning, I got up early, it was around 6:00 a.m. and the sun was starting to show its face. There were plenty of windows in the house, and with the curtains drawn back it gets very bright in here. I wandered into Olivia's room to check on her, watch her sleep and listen to her breathe. How many guys would have left a woman by now if they had been together for over five months and still haven't had sex? Quite a few of them, I'm sure. The fact that she still had her virginity at twenty- seven years old only told me that this young lady was not going to just ***settle*** for any man. He would ***have*** to be worthy of her love and affection.

I laid on her bed next to her, just watching her sleep. She woke very briefly to turn over, facing me. I rubbed her back gently and pulled back the hair that was on her face. I didn't want to wake her; I just wanted to lay there and look at her. I was in a trance as I looked at this beautiful young lady. Eventually, she woke up to me staring at her. Her beautiful eyes opened wide, and she let out a few soft, sexy wake up moans.

Olivia: "Hi, baby." She wipes her eyes.

Me: "Good morning, beautiful. I wasn't trying to wake you. I just wanted to look at you for a little bit before I went to work."

Olivia: "I kind of knew you were here after I rolled over to face you. Is it time for you to leave for work already? I can get up and make you a nice breakfast before you go. I don't want you going to work on an empty stomach."

Me: "I'm going to leave shortly. Stay in bed, don't get up. I can grab a couple of breakfast sandwiches on the way to work. I've got to grab a few supplies from the lumber yard anyways. I didn't mean to wake you, honey."

Olivia: "I can't fall back asleep now. Will you call me before you're on your way home?"

Me: "Sure. And let me know if there's anything you need while I'm out."

Olivia: "Ok, Lover. I'll see you soon."

I arrived at the job site, the house that was just up over the hill from my house. I was framing the walls on the second floor. I didn't have my guys working today. I can handle this alone. I've done it many times. I did have the crew working tomorrow to help set the roof rafters. As I was working, I was picturing Olivia here with me, helping out in her work boots, tight jeans and her very own tool belt. She mentioned before that she wanted to learn how to build walls with me. We would work well together.

It was a nice day to be working outside; not too hot yet. I was sure that I would be home before it got to that point. I could see my house from here since I was working on the second level. A few hours into framing, and I had pretty much finished up the walls on the second floor. I was excited because now the roof assembly can be built. It had been a very productive couple of hours. I called Olivia and told her that I was on my way home and asked her if she needed anything; she didn't.

I pulled in the driveway, got out of my truck, and walked around the place a bit. I wanted to make sure that no branches had broken off of the trees, and make sure the yard was free of any obstructions because I was going to mow the lawn later. I walked in the house and yelled *"Honey, I'm home* ".

Olivia: "I'm in here, Lover."

Me: "In where?" I tried to follow the voice.

I walked down the hall towards my music room; that's where my bedroom and bathroom are. I figured that maybe she was in the bathroom taking a bubble bath. As I walked by my bedroom, I caught something out of the corner of my eye. There she was, laying spread eagle on my bed with her legs spread wide apart, and she was playing with her completely shaved pussy.

Olivia: "I figured that since you won't sleep in your own bed on your own, I'd give you a reason to want to be in it."

Me: "Damn baby, you look incredible. I love the shaved pussy on you. I'm completely beside myself right now. I need some pictures of this. ***Holy shit, that's hot!*** "

Olivia: "It's time, sweetheart. Time to take this cherry from me. Yes?"

Me: "It would be an absolute pleasure. I've longed to make love to you, Olivia. I promise to be very gentle with you, my love."

She told me to take off my clothes and lay on top of her. We both loved to kiss, so that's what we did for the first few minutes. Of course, I got very hard, very fast.

Olivia: "Honey, I'm very scared to take this step, so please be very gentle with me. Promise me that you'll stop if it starts to hurt."

Me: "Honey, I will not hurt you. If you're not completely sure that you want to do this right now, then we don't have to. I won't be mad, I promise."

Olivia: "Baby, I have been dying to make love to you. Haven't you been craving it too?"

Me: "Yes, honey, very much so. This is a huge step for you. You know that, right? I love and respect you enough to wait on this if you want."

Olivia: "I'm in love with you, Julian, and there's nothing that would mean more to me than losing my virginity to the man that I want to spend the rest of my life with. Ease it in very slowly, baby. Let me get a feel for it first. And please don't be disappointed at how terrible I am in bed."

I eased it in, very slowly, as we kept kissing. She flinched at first, but she also knew that I wasn't going to shove it all in, and that put her mind at ease. She spread her legs a little farther apart and took some more of my cock in. As expected, she was very tight and breathing heavily. When it sounded like she was crying, I stopped and pulled out.

Me: "Honey, does it hurt? Do you want me to stop?"

Olivia: "No, baby. Don't you dare stop now. I've waited my whole life for this. I love you so much."

Me: "I love you too, babe."

Olivia: "Talk to me. Talk to me through the whole thing, sweetheart. Put your cock back in and kiss me. I need you to tell me how much you love me. Tell me that you want to spend the rest of your life with me, and that I will never be without you. ***Ooh, not so much, baby!*** "

Me: "Honey, you have to know by now how much I love you. You're the most beautiful lady treading this earth, and we ***will*** be spending the rest of our lives together. Being without each other is not an option."

She was moaning quite loudly now, and she would push against my stomach if it was too much for her. I found it very sexy that she loved to talk and kiss while making love. I much preferred it that way.

Olivia: "A little more, baby. Give me a little more. It's going to be quite a while before I can take all that in. So, please be patient with me."

Me: "Does it hurt, my love?"

Olivia: "Yes, a little. But I want to do this for you, for us."

We were about twenty minutes into making love when she told me to stop. I pulled out and nibbled on the side of her neck and ear lobe. She was scratching my back and moving her body like we were still making love.

Me: "Are you ok, babe?"

Olivia: "Put your cock back inside me, sweetheart. You can go a little faster this time, but please don't go any deeper."

I put it back in and she grabbed my ass with both hands and started moving her body. Her moaning wasn't as tense as it was before, but she was still very cautious. As soon as she started moving her ass a little faster, I could tell that she was on the verge of having an orgasm, as was I. I had been holding back, waiting for her to squirt first. She let out a few loud squeals and squirted all over my cock. Now that she had climaxed, it was my turn. I felt myself starting to cum.

Me: "Honey, I don't want to pull out. I really don't."

Olivia: "Well then don't pull out, baby. Give it to me, all of it. This is all yours now and I really want those seeds. If you love me, then don't you dare pull out. Cum in me, honey."

That was the first time we made love, and her first time, ever. We kissed and snuggled for at least an hour before we decided to get out of bed. We did a lot of talking afterwards as we laid there.

Me: "I love you, Olivia. It felt amazing making love to you. You are the most precious thing in my life."

Olivia: "I always knew that the first time I made love was going to feel incredible. And to top it off, I just made beautiful love with the man of my dreams. I love you with all my heart, Julian, forever."

Olivia and I sat at the dining room table and had a smoke afterwards. All she had on was her short, silky mini robe, and she looked very sexy wearing it.

Me: "So, honey, why did you shave your pussy? Don't get me wrong, I think it's totally sexy."

Olivia: "Well, you did mention to me that you thought it would look sexy on me, so I did it for you. And besides, you shave your whole cock area, which looks fucking hot, by the way."

Me: "So, are you really ok with what just happened in the bedroom? No regrets?"

Olivia: "None whatsoever, baby. Sweetheart, I'm very much in love with you, and I know that you're in love with me. I've been wanting to make love to you for so long, and I am sorry that it took me this long to finally do it. I was very nervous. I didn't want you to be unhappy with my performance."

Me: "Baby, you did great, really. I'm not just saying that."

Olivia: "I do need to know something though, and please be honest."

Me: "Honey, I'm always honest with you. You should know that."

Olivia: "Did you really want to cum inside me, or did you do it because you felt like it was the thing to do? Or was it already too late when you pulled out?"

Me: "I wanted to cum inside you. That wasn't an accident, babe. I love you that much."

Olivia: "Even knowing that I could get pregnant?"

Me: "Yes, even knowing that you could get pregnant."

Olivia: "Are you trying to get me pregnant? Do you really love me that much?"

Me: "Yes, and yes."

Olivia: "Oh, honey, I would ***love*** to have your baby, ***our*** baby. That would mean so much to me."

Me: "You know what that means though, right?"

Olivia: "Umm...making love every night? Bring it on, sweetheart. I will try my best to get better at it every time."

Me: "You are so adorable, Olivia. I can't imagine my life without you."

Olivia was absolutely glowing now that we've made love. Since she now knows that I'm trying to get her pregnant, she is feeling bliss so divine. Olivia is an only child, and she has mentioned to me that she would love to have a baby girl someday. She even has the baby's name picked out already.

While it was still daylight, we decided to take a walk. We just love walking hand in hand, and lately I've been going with her when she goes grocery shopping, just so we can hold hands in public. Whenever we go anywhere, she always wears the sexiest, tightest pants because she knows that I'll be squeezing her ass. She has also gotten into the habit of rubbing my crotch, regardless of who's around. That's our own kinky version of foreplay, which lasts all day.

Olivia: "Honey, how would you feel if I got my clit and nose pierced? Would you entertain that?"

Me: "That would look ultra-sexy on you, honey. Now you ***have*** to get it done." She chuckled.

Olivia: "Anything for you, my precious love."

Olivia lit us both a smoke as we made our way back home. She was throwing me hints that she was still horny and wanted to make love again. I'm quite sure that she knows that since we finally did make love, all we're going to do is have sex all the time, especially since I told her that I wanted to get her pregnant.

Me: "So, now that we've made love, are you going to go on birth control, honey?" She chuckled.

Olivia: "Yes. I have my own version of birth control, and it's called *"don't you dare pull out"*. Did that answer your question, ***smart ass?*** "

Later that night, after dinner, we sat outside on the swing waiting for the deer to come by for their apples. We spotted them off in the distance, and they were getting closer. Olivia and I walked towards them with the bushel of apples and started throwing them their way. Olivia was so excited that the baby deer came back to see her. We lucked out this time because we were actually able to hand feed them. Olivia was very nervous at first, actually being that close to them, but when she heard the baby deer making sounds, it warmed up her heart, and her fear of them was completely gone.

It was getting late, and I had to get some sleep. So, I got washed up and went to lay on my bed. Olivia gave me a kiss, told me that she loved me, and headed down the hall towards her apartment.

Me: "Young lady, get your sweet ass back here. From now on, in this bed, is where we're ***both*** sleeping."

Olivia: "I was waiting for you to say that to me, sweetheart. Can I interest you in some love making, or are you too tired?"

Me: “I will never be too tired to make love to you, honey. I would wake up out of a coma just to make love to you. Ok, maybe that’s a morbid example, but I think you get the picture.”

Olivia:” Now that I’ve finally felt you inside me, I have the feeling that I’m going to develop a constant craving for your cock. I mean, after all, you ***are*** trying to get me pregnant.”

Chapter 4 – Sweet Olivia's Rush

A couple of weeks had passed, and I was at work thinking about my sweet Olivia, as I usually do. The home build was coming along nicely. The roof is all done thanks to a few close friends of mine, and the masons were there finishing up with the white Italian blocks all around the house. The place was starting to look stunning. It was around noon when I got home, and Olivia was finishing up the laundry. She really loved wearing her sexy maid's outfit for me when she was doing chores. I was quite alright with that, and the best part about it is, she never wears panties or a bra when she's home.

Me: "Honey, as much as I love watching you strut around the house like that, you need to change into something more casual because we'll be out in public."

Olivia: "Yeah? Where are we going?"

Me: "We're going to buy you a car."

Olivia: "***Are you kidding me?*** "She got all excited.

Me: "No, I'm not. So please change out of that sexy outfit before I get some impure thoughts."

Olivia: "Can we take the red car? The one in the garage?"

Me: "If you would like, yes. Do you have your driver's license?"

Olivia: "I do."

Me: "Good, then you can drive."

Olivia: "***Are you serious, honey?*** You'll let me drive that?"

Me: "I don't see why not, and I can't wait to see what you look like behind the wheel of that car."

It's a bright racing red 1981 Camaro Z/28 that I restored a couple of years back. A very sharp looking car. She got in the car, warmed it up and pulled it out of the garage. If I told you right now that she looked incredibly hot and sexy in that Z/28, that would be an understatement. I told her to leave the car running and get out so I could take some pictures of her with it. She did several sexy poses for me, and then we got in the car, and we were off. I don't know what she was used to driving but this car has a lot of power under the hood. She sensed that right off the bat and was a little nervous driving it. I built a high-performance Chevy 327 for it and beefed up the transmission. So, when it shifted between gears the rear tires would chirp, and she didn't know how to react to that.

Olivia: "***Holy shit, honey!*** Is it supposed to squeal the tires like that? What am I doing wrong?"

Me: "It's fine, baby. You're doing great. It has a high-performance transmission in it. Turn on this side road and give it some throttle. Get a feel for it. As long as you respect the car you will never have any problems driving it."

Olivia: "Honey, I'm scared of this thing. I don't know if I can handle it."

Me: "Sure you can, babe. Just get familiar with how it responds and respect the power it has."

She gave it more throttle and held the steering wheel tighter. It took her a little bit to get used to it, but she was very at ease with it, and suddenly, she liked the way it drove and handled. The car drove like it was on rails and hugged the road nicely. She was getting very comfortable with it after about twenty minutes of driving around. She looked for straight aways so she could hammer the throttle down a bit. We pulled up to a stop light next to one of those rice burner cars. The guy looked over and saw Olivia behind the wheel and gave her a thumbs up.

Olivia: “Honey, is he looking to race me? What do I do?"

Me: “Just drive normal. You don't have enough time in this car to be out drag racing people. I'm sure you will be more than adequate to race in time, my love."

Olivia: “I love this car, baby. Thank you so much for letting me drive it. It's so beautiful. I bet you're very proud to own it."

Me: “I am. I only drive it on the weekends from time to time. Take a right at the next light and drive down until you see a black SUV for sale on the side of the road. I called the guy and told him that we were on our way, so he’s expecting us.”

She saw the SUV, and we pulled over. We got out and started looking it over. It was a nice-looking ride; an older Chevy Blazer, very clean and well kept. And it was a four-wheel drive. The guy came out of the house and walked towards us with the keys. Olivia liked the way the SUV looked and loved the color. It had aftermarket chrome rims, and wider than factory performance tires on it.

Me: “Hello Pete, I called you earlier today about looking at the vehicle."

Pete: "You're Julian, right?"

Me: "That's me, and this is Olivia."

Pete: "Hello, Olivia, it's a pleasure to meet both of you. Say, that's a very sharp Camaro Z/28 you've got there. You don't see those every day."

Me: "Yeah, she likes it just fine. We're looking to get her something that she can drive every day to do her running around with."

Pete: "Well, here's the keys, take it for a ride. I'm the original owner and I've taken great care of it, as you will see with all the maintenance receipts."

Olivia got in the driver's seat, and we went down the road a bit. She said that she liked the way it felt and drove, and it had all the power accessories.

Olivia: "Honey, I don't have enough money saved up to buy this. This is way out of my price range."

Me: "Do you like it?"

Olivia: "Yes, I like it but..."

Me: "Well, then I'm buying it for you, problem solved."

Olivia: "No, honey, don't buy this for me, please."

Me: "Olivia, I want you in something safe and reliable, and I want to do this for you. I've got the cash to buy this and that's what we're going to do."

We got back to the guy's house. I paid him cash for it, got the title to it, and told him that we would be back in a few days with plates for it, and drive it out of there. She asked me to drive the Z/28 home. We got back home, and I pulled the car into the garage. We were walking towards the house, and she started crying. I grabbed her and held her.

Me: "Honey, what's wrong? You should be happy right now. What's wrong, baby?"

She didn't answer me. She just kept crying and holding me tighter.

Me: "Honey, tell me what's wrong. I figured you'd be very happy about this."

Olivia: "I am happy, baby, very happy. So happy that I don't know how to absorb it all. You've done so much for me. You've made me feel these incredible feelings; feelings I didn't even know existed. I love you so much that it would crush me to ever lose you. Please don't ever leave me. ***Please!*** "

Her crying intensified and got louder; she held me even tighter. I started to break down myself. It was very hard to get my words out. I have obviously brought out feelings in her that she had never experienced before. I was still wrapping myself around all that had happened since I met her. I, too, was experiencing feelings that I thought were unheard of, or what they really meant.

Me: "Baby, look at me. Look at me. ***Listen!*** When you came into my life it was the best thing that's ever happened to me. I had no idea that love could feel this way. It would crush me to lose you too, I swear. This life that we have together is exactly how I saw it in my dreams. You are a lady in full, and I absolutely adore you. There is nothing in this world that I wouldn't do for you, for us. You complete me, and that's the only way I can say it. You are my life, baby."

Olivia: "I love you, my handsome man. I am yours forever, I promise. ***I promise you, baby!*** "

Me: "I love you too, Olivia, and I believe you. I am yours forever as well."

We collected our thoughts and finally made it into the house where we had a smoke and something to drink. I walked up to her, lifted her chin up with my finger, looked into those beautiful eyes and kissed her. I went to pull away and she wouldn't let me. She kissed me back and we engaged in one of our infamous five-minute kisses. Once I started kissing her, I found it very hard to stop. She had the kind of lips that I could kiss forever, especially since she loved kissing as much as I did, and she was such a great kisser.

Me: "Would you like to go get some ice cream, honey? I've been craving it all day."

Olivia: "Yeah, that sounds great. Can we take the Z/28?"

Me: "We sure can, but only if you drive us there."

Olivia: "Of course I will, baby. Because that was my next question." She chuckled and wiped her eyes.

Me: "You really love driving this car, don't you?"

Olivia: "Oh yeah, but I'm still a little nervous behind the wheel. I'm sure I'll get better in time, depending on how much you let me drive it."

We got in the car, and she fired it up. The car rumbled and shook a little. She let it warm up, and we were off. I told her to take the expressway so she could weave in and out of cars with it and get used to its handling. At one time she had us going eighty-five miles per hour when she was passing another car, but she quickly let up on the throttle. She was beginning to respect the car and that was good. We exited the expressway and got off right next to the ice cream place. We pulled into the parking lot and there were quite a few people there sitting at picnic tables. Needless to say, when we got out of the car and started walking hand in hand, she attracted attention, especially getting out of that Z/28. We got our ice cream cones and found a table to sit at. We were sitting there just watching people look at the car. I've had it for about ten years, but it didn't look like that when I got it. I've done a lot of work on it, and even painted it myself.

Olivia: “You must love driving that car around and flaunting it, huh, baby?"

Me: “I don't know if it's flaunting it as much as it is appreciating it. But with you behind the wheel I get to flaunt both of you at the same time. And ***that***, I am certainly proud of."

Olivia: “***Ooh!*** I just had a passing thought; a very dirty one, actually.”

Me: “What?"

Olivia: “Oh, nothing, honey.” She chuckled.

Me: “Tell me, Lover.”

Olivia: “I was just imagining what it would have been like if you had popped my cherry on the hood of that car."

Me: "I actually had that same exact thought myself; I swear. I would have had to re-paint the hood."

We both laughed after that statement. It was kind of sexy that she had the same exact thought.

Olivia: "Yeah, you're right. I'm sure sex juice probably wouldn't be the best thing for the paint."

She started licking her ice cream cone very slowly and swirled her tongue in and around it.

Olivia: "Oh, I'm sorry, honey. Am I distracting you? Huh, baby?"

She shoved the cone in and out of her mouth as if she was performing oral sex on it. She looked around really quick to see if anyone saw her doing that. Several people did, actually. I just shook my head. But I was very proud and honored to be with such a beautiful lady. She was the sexiest chambermaid I had ever seen. We finished our ice cream and got in the car. One guy asked Olivia to light the tires up. There were even several little kids telling Olivia to do a burn out. She fired it up and put it in gear, drove very slowly in the parking lot, which had a lot of little stones on it. She turned onto the main road and hit the throttle, breaking the rear tires loose, and all you heard was the squealing of the rear tires as the car shifted from gear to gear. There was a trail of smoke behind us. She got back on the expressway, and we drove for about forty- five- minutes, way passed the exit we needed to get off at to go home.

Olivia: "Honey, this car gets me horny, so we should probably get back home before I soak the seat." She chuckled.

Me: "Well, I'm glad you like driving it as much as I do. Wait until you drive the Trans Am. That's ***really*** going to make you cum in your pants."

Olivia: "You'll let me drive that one too? ***Seriously, baby?"***

Me: "Yes, not for a while though. That car has quite a bit more muscle under the hood. That one will definitely scare you. But it's a manual transmission, so you'll need some lessons first."

Olivia: "I think I'll stick to this one where I don't have to shift it all the time."

Me: "Do we need anything while we're out?"

Olivia: "I can't think of anything off the top of my head. Actually, we do need to grab some sex lube if you plan on stretching me out with that big dick of yours."

We got home, and she pulled the car into the garage. We grabbed some wine and went out on the deck and sat on the two-person swing, just rocking away, and holding each other. She laid her head on my shoulder and put her hand between my legs. She wasn't trying to get me excited. She was subconsciously doing that while we talked.

Olivia: "I really enjoyed driving that car today, honey. I'm sure driving the SUV will be boring compared to the Z/28. And I want to thank you so much for getting me the Blazer, honey. I love you ***so*** much, you have no idea."

Me: "If it's as much as I love you, then trust me, I have an idea. The fireworks are tonight so, did you still want to go?"

Olivia: "Umm, why don't we stay home tonight? I'll make us a picnic basket, and we can lay a blanket on the lawn and stare out into the sky all night. Ok, baby? Keep it simple? Maybe we'll be able to see some of the fireworks from here."

Me: "That sounds great. And besides we can see the fireworks from here."

Olivia: "We can? Really? That will be awesome."

Me: "Yeah. I never watch them because once you've seen one firework display, you've pretty much seen them all. We should have gotten more wine while we were out earlier, I think we're running low."

Olivia: "I'll run out and grab some if you trust me driving your truck."

Me: "Of course I do, honey. Just don't go off roading with it. My wallet's on the table."

Olivia: "No. I got it. It's the least I can do."

She got in the truck and headed out. Shortly after she left, she pulled over to the side of the road for a few minutes. She looked at my carpenter's tool pouch on the front seat, and there were also a couple of power tools on the floor in front of the passenger seat. She picked several of the tools up and just felt them, knowing that my handprints and sweat were all over them. She got emotional and kissed them before she put them back and rubbed her hand on them softly. These are the tools that I use every day to build houses. She said to herself and out loud: "*I love you so much, baby.*"

She reached the liquor store, made a couple of other quick stops, and then she headed back home. It was going to get dark soon and she wanted to make some food for tonight under the stars. I took a shower while Olivia was out getting wine and running around. She returned home and got out of the truck. I walked outside.

Me: "You know, there's not many things sexier than seeing a beautiful lady driving a truck. Unless she's driving a red Z/28, of course." She smiled from ear to ear.

Olivia: "Keep it up, baby, flattery will get you laid every time." She gave me a wink.

It was starting to get dark out, so Olivia made up a couple of snack trays while I grabbed a blanket to spread on the ground. I grabbed a second blanket in case it got chilly out later. I turned on the deck lights, which lit up quite a bit of the yard where we would be laying out. I removed the cork from the wine and grabbed two wine glasses. Olivia got changed really quick, grabbed the tray of food, and joined me outside. I was lying on the blanket and looked up to see that Olivia was wearing crotchless leggings, a sweatshirt with no bra, and obviously no panties, as usual. She looked and smelled incredible.

I poured us some wine and she lit us both up a smoke. We were both sitting up on the blanket enjoying our wine and smokes, listening to the sound of the crickets chirping and the frogs by the creek nearby. After we finished our first glass of wine we laid down on the blanket and snuggled.

Olivia: "Honey, this is so romantic, I just love it to pieces. I have my sexy, strong man by my side and there's nothing in this world I love more."

Me: "And you, my love, being next to me on this peaceful starlit night is all I need. It's the perfect ending to a wonderful day."

Olivia: "The day hasn't ended yet baby, and I have the ***perfect*** ending for it."

We heard the fireworks going off in the distance and we could see them as well. I laid her on her back and told her to just relax and enjoy the show. She laid there and watched the fireworks light up the sky while I got on my knees and put my head right between her legs. It only took five minutes to get her off.

Olivia: "***Ooh!*** You kinky man. ***Wow, baby!*** You're so good with that tongue. ***Yes, honey, yes!*** "

Needless to say, she squirted all over my face. That was a first for her, and now that I know she likes it, maybe that will become part of our love making. We laid under the stars for a little bit longer, and then headed inside for the night. We went to bed, in ***our bed!*** She no longer sleeps in her apartment. We didn't make love, but we did spend a little time kissing and holding each other.

The next morning when we woke, the sun was already lighting up the sky. She made us breakfast, and then we went outside. I asked her if she wanted to pull the Z/28 out of the garage so we could wash it. She did, of course. She was wearing super tight shorts that were very thin and riding the crack of her ass. And of course, no underwear. She just had on a thin T-shirt, practically see through. We started washing the car and spent more time spraying each other with the hose. Her clothes were completely see- through now.

We washed it really quick, changed into some dry clothes, and went for a drive. Of course, Olivia wanted to drive. She took it out on the expressway and hammered the throttle a bit. I was going to put my hand between her legs, but I didn't want to distract her from driving. We drove for about a half hour, and then got off the expressway. We went to a local diner for lunch. As usual, Olivia looked stunning, especially getting out of that car. She got noticed very fast. I watched her strut and wiggle her sweet ass as we walked into the place. Over lunch we talked about last night under the stars. We also discussed when we were going to get license plates for her Blazer and go pick it up. I told her we would go first thing Monday morning, before I went to work.

On the way home we drove by the house up over the hill that I was working on. She pulled up the long driveway, and when we parked in front of it, she just looked at it in complete awe. We got out and walked around the place. The hole was being dug for the in-ground swimming pool. The yard was huge, and all fenced in with black steel fencing. The crews have been there all along working their asses off. We were just about ready to start on the interior of the house and start painting the walls. When you first walk in, you walk into a huge room with a thirty-foot cathedral ceiling. That was the living room. I gave her the full tour, even though it was still just a shell of a house. But still, she was very impressed with it.

Olivia: "***Wow!*** This place is huge, honey. It looks beautiful. You did a great job and I'm sure the people buying it are going to love it."

Me: "Yeah, I'm sure the couple moving in will love it to pieces and spend the rest of their lives here."

Chapter 5 – My Sexy Helper

Monday morning rolled around, and we went to the DMV to get plates for her Blazer. We drove out to put the plates on it and get it home. We gave it a good wash and cleaned the interior really good. It was actually a very sharp ride. She really enjoyed it on the way home. I asked her to come to work with me for a couple of hours. I wanted her opinion on a few interior designs. The homeowner left all that up to me to design, but I wanted a lady's opinion on it. That is where Olivia discovered she had a hidden talent. She had a natural knack for interior design and ended up being very proficient at it.

I surprised her with her very own tool belt and work boots. She was ecstatic and wanted to get her hands dirty. She helped me with the framing in the garage out back. I got her familiar with a few power tools but watched her very carefully as she used them. I got her proficient in cutting lumber for me and using a tape measure and speed square. She looked sexy as ever with her cut off jean shorts, tool belt and work boots. I even bought her a red and black checkered shirt like mine. It was very hard to concentrate with her around, but I loved having her on the job site, as did my co-workers.

We worked for a few hours, and then went out to grab a bite to eat before we went home. It was very hot outside, so Olivia decided to lie out in the sun while I went into my music room and laid down some more guitar tracks. The window in my music room had a great view of the yard, and of course, that's where Olivia was laying out, completely nude. She wanted to go to work with me tomorrow so she could do some more thinking on the kitchen and bathroom layouts as far as the ceramic tile colors, and the style of the cabinets. The place was coming together very fast. I should have it done way ahead of schedule. My sexy maid was turning out to be quite the carpenter's assistant.

I wanted to get to bed early tonight because I planned on getting up earlier than usual in the morning to run some errands before work. So, I went to bed, and she said she would be in soon after she watched her cooking show.

Morning came, and we got up and hit the shower together. Nothing sexual happened in the shower, but we did wash each other's bodies, which was amazing foreplay. We got dressed, had breakfast, and then I gave her a kiss goodbye and ran off to do some errands. She showed up at the job site with some lunch, and she was wearing her tight cut off jean shorts with the checkered shirt that I had bought her, along with her cute little work boots. We ate really quick, and then I brought her inside to meet someone. It was the lady who was doing all of the ordering for me when it came time to buy furnishings for the house, or pretty much any material I needed.

Me: "Olivia, this Bonnie. I want you to work with her and come up with a list of paints, tiles and appliances so she can order them for me. Just imagine if this was your house and you were ordering them for yourself. I trust your judgement, so just walk around, and tell her what you want, and she'll get them delivered here for me. I was thinking of a nice center island in the kitchen somewhere so try to figure out where you'd want it. Order all of the window and bedroom furnishings, and just go room by room. I'll be outside working in the garage if you need me. Oh, and before I forget, honey, order me some fluorescent lighting for the garage. Six pieces should be plenty. Have fun, Lover."

Olivia: "Ok, bye baby."

Olivia looked through the product catalog and came up with a huge list of materials that she thought would look beautiful in the house. She ordered all of the bedroom and living room furnishings. When I build houses, I never build them fully furnished, but this was an exception. This house will have a lot of money and time put into it so it will fetch a hefty price. I already have a couple in mind who would just love to own it. Money is no option for them.

Olivia: "Honey, if you're done with me here, I'd like to get home and finish my chores if that's ok."

Me: "Of course, my love, and thank you so much for your help. You've saved me a lot of time and thinking. Drive safe, I love you, girl."

Olivia: "I love you too, honey, see you soon. I thought I might make you lasagna tonight for dinner. I'm swinging by the grocery store on my way home to get the ingredients."

She headed home, and two hours later, I headed home. She had dinner on the table, lasagna, my favorite, with a nice salad and homemade bread. My baby loves to cook. I went to wash up really quick, and when I got to the bathroom, on the counter, was a card and small box that had my name on it. I read the card, which was beautiful, and opened the box. It was a stunning white gold bracelet that read "*Maid to Love you* ". I was beside myself, at a complete loss for words. I cleaned up and quickly put it on my wrist. I walked out to the dining room where Olivia was sitting at the table having her smoke. I was so touched by this that it was hard to speak.

Me: "Baby, I love it. I will never take it off. It's so beautiful."

Olivia: "I'm glad you like it. Please don't wear it to work, it might get all scratched up. And when you're not working, I'd love for you to always have it on."

She walked towards me, and I grabbed her and gave her a nice, long kiss. I looked into her beautiful eyes, and I was lost in our world. My emotions calmed down and we finally sat at the table to have dinner. Gifts don't have to be expensive to make someone feel happy and loved. The littlest effort is all it takes. My lady knew me like the back of her hand, and she also knew how much this bracelet meant to me. I adored her beyond words. There was no doubt in my mind that we were made for each other.

Olivia: "I had that made for you, my love, as you can tell by the words on it."

Me: "I love it, and that's a great choice of words. It's perfect."

Olivia: "Now we both have bracelets from each other. Being in love is such a beautiful feeling. Isn't it?"

We ate our dinner; it was delicious as always. She bought a cake for dessert, triple chocolate. That went well with a cup of coffee. After dinner we went out on the deck and had our coffee and a smoke. We were sitting on the futon listening to music.

Olivia: "I can tell you really appreciate life and all of its beautiful creatures. That is so attractive. I just adore the man you are, honey. I feel so bad for animals that are left out in the elements to fend for themselves. They don't have all the luxuries that we humans do."

Me: "Have you ever shot a gun before?"

Olivia: "***Oh no!*** I would be afraid to pull the trigger. I would worry that it might snap back and hit me in the face. Have you?"

Me: "I have. In fact, I have several shotguns and rifles. Sometimes I'll set up targets and just blow off a few rounds to let off some steam."

Olivia: "Honey, will you light me a smoke please?"

Me: "Sure. Would you like something to drink? Iced tea, maybe?"

Olivia: "That would be great, thank you."

Me: "So, do you love being out on your own in your own little apartment?"

Olivia: "Yes, but I'd rather be living on ***your*** side of the house with you, since I'm always there."

Me: "That's what I was getting at. You read my mind."

Olivia: "Oh baby, I would love that more than ***anything***." She got misty eyed.

She hugged me and buried her head in my chest as I rubbed her back and the back of her head. I didn't want her to think that she was just my casual sex partner.

Olivia: "I love you so much. You really know how to make me

feel loved and wanted. You have no idea how much I've wanted this to happen."

Me: "Well, it was time to do this. We sleep in the same bed now, and besides, you're over on my side of the house most of the time anyways."

Olivia: "I feel so honored, blessed, and lucky to have you in my life, honey. I wish I could put it in words, I really do."

A week or so had passed, and the home project was making great progress. All the interior appliances had arrived, as well as the ceramic tiles, marble countertops, and paint. I had a painting crew come in to knock that off really quick, while my crew and I focused on laying down all the ceramic tiles. My sweet helper Olivia was joining in on the fun. She was a very quick learner, and she enjoyed working with me. It gave her a break from cleaning and folding clothes. All of my workers were quite aware of who Olivia was, and they also acted like gentlemen around her. I'm sure they were all checking her out from time to time, and that's ok. It's harmless, and I knew that my sweet Olivia would never intentionally attract attention to herself. She wasn't the kind of lady who just ***had*** to be noticed. She was very much on the shy side, and to me, that made her even more attractive.

Olivia: "I know why you asked me help with the floor tiles, honey."

Me: "Yeah? Why is that?"

Olivia: "Is it because you love having me on my knees? C'mon honey, you can tell me, I'm a big girl."

Me: "Don't be silly girl, of course I do." I winked at her.

Olivia: "How much longer do you think it will take before this place is ready to live in? It has to be very close to that now, right?"

Me: "About two weeks, give or take, minus the landscaping of course. The grass will take a while to grow yet. I have the asphalt crew coming in this weekend to do the driveway."

The house sat back quite a bit from the road. You would have to be looking for it as you drove by, or you would never see it through the tree lines. Olivia worked at home for the rest of the week. I was finishing up on the ceramic tiles when she sent me a video of her masturbating outside while lying on the blanket. She knew fully well that I would spend the rest of the workday thinking about that.

By the end of the day, I finally had the floors all done, with a lot of help from friends and contractors, and now all the appliances can be set into place and hooked up. Olivia's ideas on the interior designs really paid off. Her choice of colors, textures and fixtures really made the place look incredibly gorgeous. All the windows were put in, and the rooms that required carpeting have all been carpeted. We could park all four of our vehicles comfortably in the living room, that's how big it is. It had been a long day, so I headed home. When I got home Olivia was lying out in the backyard completely naked, smoking a cigarette and laying on her belly.

Olivia: "Hi baby, I missed you. I'm glad you're home. I know it sounds selfish, but I hate not being with you all day."

Me: "I feel the same way, Olivia. It's very hard to leave you in the morning. You're getting very tan, girl. It looks very sexy on you."

When she was done laying on the blanket, we both went inside to shower together. We loved showering together as often as we could. After that, she put on a pot of coffee, and we sat at the table for a little while talking about her Blazer and how she really enjoyed driving it. And of course, we had to talk about her driving the Z/28 again. I told her that we should go for a nice cruise, only this time we were taking the Trans Am. She was excited to finally go for a ride in it.

So, we headed out to the garage and got into the Trans Am. I fired it up and let it warm up a bit, and then we were off. I hopped on the expressway, shifted it down a gear and hammered the throttle. It set her right back in her seat, and she was terrified. She reached over and grabbed my thigh and squeezed it tight. I wasn't going to get carried away, but from time to time I did like to open it up a bit. Maybe now was not one of those times.

Olivia: "***Damn, baby!*** This car scares the ***shit out of me!*** I trust your driving, sweetheart, but I have to be honest. Being inside this car makes a ***little nervous.***"

Me: "It's nasty, for sure, but I respect it's power."

Olivia: "It's a gorgeous car, honey. Both of your cars are gorgeous."

Me: "Everything in my life is gorgeous, babe, especially you. I have exquisite taste, no doubt."

Olivia: "It really flatters me that you find me so attractive, you make me blush."

We arrived at the ice cream parlor and we both got chocolate and vanilla swirl on a cone. We preferred soft ice cream over frozen. As usual, the car got a lot of looks, and this time we were eating our ice cream in the car. It looked like it might rain soon, so I wanted to get the car back home and into the garage. I asked her if she wanted to learn how to drive it and she said no. She preferred the Z/28, and I respected that. The Trans Am is way too much car for her to handle right now.

Olivia: "Oh, honey, before I forget again to tell you, the garbage disposal is making a humming noise when I turn it on. I wonder if something might be stuck inside there."

Me: "Please tell me that you didn't stick your hand down inside it. Don't ever, ever do that, honey. If that thing kicks on with your hand in there, it will tear your hand to shreds."

Olivia: "Don't worry, sweetheart. I wasn't about to put my hand down there."

Me: "Good. I'll check it out when we get home."

Once we got home, Olivia made us a drink while I checked out the garbage disposal. There was definitely something jammed down inside there. I was able to break it free using an Allen head socket. I showed Olivia exactly what I was doing so she would know what to do if it ever jammed up again. One thing about Olivia; she loves to learn new things, and I love that about her. While I had my toolbox out, I was going to show Olivia how to swap out a ceiling light fixture. The one in the dining room is quite old and out of style. I purchased a new one several days ago, and since I had my sexy helper with me, it was the perfect time to change it. I explained to her, step by step, how to properly do it without getting zapped.

Olivia: "Honey, if I touch these wires, are they going to jolt me?"

Me: "No, babe. As long as the wall switch is off going to the fixture, there is no juice going to it, providing that there's not another switch feeding the light, which there is not."

Olivia: "So, black to black, white to white, and green to ground?"

Me: "You got it, baby. Just make sure that after you wire nut them together, you wrap them in electrical tape. We'll throw some fresh bulbs in it as well."

Olivia had the new fixture wired and mounted, and now it was time to turn the switch on to see if she had done it correctly. There is no doubt in my mind that she did it correctly. She did great.

Me: "Well, look at that, young lady. You did a fantastic job. You can add that to your resume' now."

Olivia: "Thank you, honey. What a difference, huh? It seems a lot brighter in this room. I really like that new fixture too, to be honest with you."

Me: "I do need to swap out the hot water heater too, but I haven't gotten a new one yet. I will go to the home improvement store tomorrow and get one."

Olivia: "Can I help you put the new one in? I've got my very own tool belt and everything." She chuckled.

Me: "Of course you can, honey. I will show you how to cut and sweat copper."

When I got home from work the next day, after Olivia and I had our dinner, she helped me unload the new water heater from the back of my truck. Before we even started eating, I hooked up a hose to the old one and started draining it. These are usually not bad installations unless you have to turn off the water coming into the house. Every water heater should have its own shut off valves, which mine did. I showed Olivia how to use a copper tubing cutter as well as where to shut off the gas valve feeding the unit. We had the new water heater swapped out in no time at all. I used a dolly to get the old one outside to my truck; Olivia helped me load it into the back of my truck. I'll just throw it in the dumpster that I have at my job site.

Olivia: "Honey, you should just put me on your payroll and let me join your crew."

Me: "You're already on my payroll, sweetie. You're the only one that gets paid under the table, for being my sexy maid. But I can tell you that sometime in the near future I'm going to need to set up some kind of office setting so you can answer any business-related phone calls and do payroll for me. How would you feel about that?"

Olivia: "I would ***love that***. You're not just teasing me, are you?"

Me: "No, honey, I am serious about this. I'm not quite ready for that just yet; but soon, I promise."

Olivia: "I can do that for you, baby. I would love to be directly involved in your business, as long as I get the *"fringe benefits"* package." She smiled and chuckled.

I figured that since we had plenty of daylight left, we may as well change the oil and filters in the cars. Olivia pulled the Z/28 out of the garage, and I guided her to drive it up on car ramps. Even though the car was on ramps, I still use jack stands under the car as a safety precaution, especially if Olivia was going to be under there. I removed the old oil filter and took out the oil drain plug. Once the oil was completely drained, Olivia installed the new filter and tightened the drain plug in the oil pan. At that point, I had Olivia back the car off the ramps onto level ground. She added the new oil into the valve cover, fired the car up for a few seconds, and then made sure the oil dipstick showed the correct amount of oil in the motor. It was the same procedure for the Trans Am, only this time I drove it on the ramps since Olivia didn't know how to drive a manual transmission. I am so proud of my precious lady. She loves doing things together, and that's what it's all about.

Olivia: "Can we take the cars for a ride, honey. ***Pretty please?*** "

Me: "Sure. I don't see why not. We'll take them down by the lake and grab a burger while we're there."

Olivia: "Sounds good to me. I do have to change my clothes though."

We changed clothes and headed out. She led the way in the Z/28, and I followed her in the Trans Am. At one time, when we were on the expressway, I pulled up next to her to see if she was interested in racing me. She just smiled and shook her head as if she was saying *"no"*. While we were out, we stopped at the *"adult"* store to grab some sex lube and kinky, skimpy outfits for my sexy lady. She loves role playing different characters for me in the bedroom. From time to time, we'll even have the camcorder on while we're making love. I have a few choice video clips on my cell phone, as does she. Needless to say, both of our cell phones are password protected.

In hindsight, us going to the *"adult"* store while we were out driving the cars, wasn't the best idea at the time. Our cars tend to attract a lot of attention, so as Olivia and I were leaving the store, there were a few people walking around the cars, checking them out. Normally, there is no harm in that, but when we were just seen exiting the *"adult"* store, and Olivia is holding a big bag of goodies, it becomes a matter of embarrassment. I guess you could even call that an invasion of privacy. On the other hand, those people were also in the market to buy something kinky, so that eased up on our embarrassment a little. But still, when you're trying to be discreet about something, it becomes a little un-nerving.

One of the couples looking at our cars was older, extremely attractive, and very polite. It was good to see that people their age still had a highly active sex life, or at least trying to keep their sex life spicey. After talking with them for a few minutes, they revealed that they were both in their mid to late sixties. The lady's name was Candace and her husband's name was Larry. I have old fashioned values and morals, so whenever I get a chance to talk with people from an older generation, I tend to listen. The other couple, who weren't with Candace and Larry, went inside the store while Larry and I were talking about the older cars. He was driving an older Chevy truck from the late 50's, so of course I took an interest in it. Candace and Olivia were standing next to the Z/28 at this time, talking amongst themselves. We ended up exchanging numbers with them before we left.

Once we got back home, after we parked the cars in the garage, we had a cup of coffee on the two-person swing. We were reflecting on our conversations with Candace and Larry.

Olivia: "I'm glad we met them, honey. Candace is someone I

could talk to for hours on end. She is so pretty. Would you agree?"

Me: "Candace is ***very*** attractive. They both look great."

Olivia: "I hope ***my*** body looks as good as hers when I'm her age. She is sixty-nine years old, honey. He is five years younger than her. I will make it a point to call her every week. I would love to have them over for dinner sometime. Yes?"

Me: "Absolutely. They're good people and it's an honor to know them."

Olivia: "She did tell me that they don't have any children. Did Larry happen to tell you that Candace did the interior in his truck?"

Me: "Really? That is very impressive. No, he did not mention that. So then, like you, she's a sexy helper."

Olivia: "You're very flattering, honey." She leans over and kisses me.

Me: "When are you going to let me tap that sweet ass of yours?"

Olivia: "Honey, I'm still trying to get use to the size of your cock. You're not exactly small, you know."

Me: "I've been very gentle with you. Have I not?"

Olivia: "You've been ***very*** gentle with me, baby. I still think that you ***love*** to hear me squeal, don't you?"

Me: "I do it all out of my love for you." She chuckled.

Olivia: "I'm sure you do. And I spread my legs for you every day, sometimes several times a day, get the living shit fucked out of me, and go to sleep very sore, all out of ***my*** love for ***you***. ***Smart ass!*** "

For the remainder of the day, Olivia and I snuggled up on the pull-out sofa. We managed to find a good DVD to watch. We were both getting tired at that point, so we decided to call it a night and nestle down in our bed. Olivia went to work with me the following morning for a few hours. She wanted to finish setting up the living room. The lamps, end tables, coffee table, and flatscreen TV were still in their boxes. The TV was going to be mounted on the wall, so that was the first thing we did. Once that was done, she focused on setting the end tables and lamps in place. While I was hooking up the plumbing for the kitchen sink, she cut down all the cardboard boxes and brought them outside to the dumpster. I really love working next to her. I'm so proud and honored that she has taken an interest in my profession. She was definitely sent to me from the Heavens.

Chapter 6 – A House Built on Dreams

We were well into August now, and finally, after a very long past two weeks, the house was pretty much finished. I had to run back up to the house to make sure there were no loose ends that I had to tie up. I asked Olivia if she wanted to ride up with me to make sure all the rooms looked presentable. She said yes, and we headed up there. It was a huge place on a huge piece of land with an inground swimming pool and a garage big enough to fit several cars in it. We pulled up the driveway, looked at it for a few minutes, and then walked in. We walked around the whole place and just admired its beauty. Marble counter tops, everywhere. Gorgeous ceramic tiles, everywhere. Beautiful chandeliers hanging from the ceilings. It has huge bedrooms, four of them, with a king-sized bed in each one. The master bedroom has his and hers matching vanities with gorgeous marble tops. I thought it was ready to show now. Under one of the kitchen cabinets was a cabinet mounted coffee maker. And just below that on the counter were two coffee cups just in case she or I wanted a cup of coffee.

Me: "Hun, do you want a cup of coffee?"

Olivia: "Yeah, I could go for one."

Me: "Well, the coffee is already brewed and there are two cups on the counter. Just fill them up for us please. There's also cream and sugar in those jars next to the cups."

She walked out into the kitchen towards the coffee maker

where there were two cups on the counter turned upside down. She turned over the first one and filled it up. When she turned over the second cup, there was a small box underneath it. She took a step back and stared at it for a few seconds, and then opened the little box up. There in front of her was the most beautiful diamond ring she had ever seen in her life. She closed her eyes for a second, and then opened them again. She wanted to be sure of what she was looking at. There were chills running down her spine as she became nervous.

Olivia: "***Umm...Julian?*** Honey, can you come here, please? What is ***this?*** "

Me: "Well, it looks to me like a diamond engagement ring with a pretty big stone in it."

Olivia: "I understand that, but who is it for?"

Me: "It's for you my love, and we are the couple moving into this beautiful house."

Olivia: "***What? Are you kidding me right now, Julian? Are you, honey?*** "

She cried uncontrollably and latched on to me. All I could do was try to keep her calm. Her body was shaking as if she was cold. I hugged her as tight as I could, and then kissed the top of her head, while rubbing her back. I did all I could to comfort her, and hearing her cry was crushing my heart, but at the same time I knew that she was crying tears of joy and not sorrow. I didn't know how else to surprise her with the ring. I did feel though that my idea was quite ingenious. There was no way on this earth that I was going to be without her for the rest of my life.

Me: “It's ok, baby. It's ok to cry."

She would not let go of me and wasn't able to talk just yet. She just hung on to me and cried. At one point I thought I was going to have to hold her up. Her knees seemed very weak. Slowly she was coming around, enough to where she made an effort to talk.

Olivia: “Oh baby, I cannot ***believe*** this. I cannot believe this is happening. I must be dreaming because this can't be happening to me."

Me: “Honey, look at me. ***Look at me!*** Are you ok now?"

Olivia: “Oh Julian, this is beyond words for me. This is the sort of thing people read about in fairy tales. Is this really happening? If I'm dreaming, please don’t wake me. ***Please, don’t!*** “

Me: “Do you like the ring?"

Olivia: “I love it, baby. It’s absolutely stunning.”

Me: “Why haven't you put it on yet?"

Olivia: “Because when I first saw it, I didn't think it was for me. I thought maybe it was for the guy's wife who's moving in here, so I didn't touch it."

Me: “Well, it is for you, my love, and I hope it’s the right size.”

I grabbed the ring from the box and took her left hand. She was staring at me with those beautiful grayish blue eyes of hers. She would not take her eyes off of mine. Her hand was shaking as I held it, trying to place the ring on it.

Me: “Olivia, I want to spend the rest of my life with you, here, in this house, in ***our*** house. Don't let me put this ring on your finger unless you are completely sure that you feel the same way."

Her eyes were piercing into mine and we both knew at that moment that this was the best thing that either of us had ever felt.

Olivia: "Put it on, baby. Yes, of course I feel the same way. I love you more than I will ever be able to tell you. You have completely changed my life in so many beautiful ways. I am beside myself right now. I wish I could say more but I can't." She cried again.

She buried her head in my chest again and I held her as long as it took to calm her down. She looked at the ring and kissed it. I wiped the tears running down her face. She held me even tighter and could not stop crying. I kept rubbing her back until she was completely calm. She certainly didn't expect ***this*** when she got here.

Olivia: "This is ***our*** house? Am I standing in my own kitchen?" She wiped her eyes.

Me: "I started building this about a year ago, in between projects, and I was going to take my sweet time building it, and for the most part, I did. And then I met you and fell in love with you. That was my motivation to finish it. I've had a lot of help from friends and contractors to get it done. I owe them a lot of beer now. I paid them all very well for their time and efforts. My biggest fear was when you came here to help me, I didn't want you to overhear the guys talking about what was ***really*** going on. That would have spoiled it. But that never happened, thankfully."

Olivia: “Oh baby, you are a man in full and you've made me the happiest lady on this planet. I'm sorry for still crying a bit, I'm just trying to get the words out. I need a little time to absorb all this. This is amazing, and you are an amazing man. I will spend the rest of my life with you, honey, I swear to it.”

Me: “It's a lot to soak in, I know. I was a basket case trying to make this all happen."

Olivia: “I love this ring, honey, it's ***stunning!*** So stunning. I love you so much, sweetheart.”

She kept looking at her ring and kissing it, along with the bracelet I got her. We walked around the house holding hands, taking it all in. I’ve waited for this moment my whole life; my true, deep love.

Me: “All these cabinets, all these fixtures, all these countertops; honey, you picked them all out yourself. The colors on the walls, the carpets; you chose them. The bedroom furnishings all look beautiful, thanks to you. There's a king size bed in every bedroom, and the dressers are simply gorgeous."

Olivia: “Well I'm sure all those beds are going to get quite the work out. Huh, baby?"

Me: “***Oh yeah, they are!*** “

Olivia: “So honey, what are you doing with the house we're in now? Are you going to sell it? That's a very nice house too."

Me: “I'm not sure yet on that. We'll have to talk about it. I will include you in my decision, of course.”

Olivia: “You never wanted a cup of coffee, ***did you?*** “

Me: “***Umm, nope!*** I smiled at her and winked.

Olivia: “You are something else, baby. I have dreamt about you my whole life, Julian. Oh baby, this is so surreal. I never thought I was worthy of feeling this happy, this is incredible. I'm having a hard time digesting it. I still can't believe this happened. You've made my day, my life, my world."

Her eyes were still watering, and she had a very hard time holding back the tears.

Me: “So what would you like to do to celebrate this day, my sweet Olivia?"

Olivia: “Why don't we go lay in one of our many beds and hold each other. I really need you to hold me right now. At least until I'm convinced that I’m not imagining this.”

Me: “Sure, babe. Let's head to the master bedroom, our new bedroom, in our new house.”

Olivia: “Lead the way, sweetheart."

I grabbed her hand and led her upstairs to our new bedroom, a huge bedroom at that. It overlooked the pool and the tree lines. We laid down and held each other tight. She was very emotional right now, and I didn’t want her to think that I wanted to have sex. I was very content with just kissing and holding her. The once hotel hottie was now my beautiful fiancé`. She was the only thing missing from my life, and now that I had her, my life felt complete. It really tugs on my heartstrings when I see how I have made this beautiful young lady as happy as she is.

A lot of my friends were already married with kids, and most of them divorced while they were still in their mid-twenties. I did not want to be like everyone else. I mean, who in the hell really likes going through a terrible divorce and fighting over custody of the kids? Certainly not me. I have done a lot of fucked up shit in my life, but there is one thing that I'm never going to fail at doing, and that is being a loyal, dedicated, and faithful husband.

Olivia: "Honey?"

Me: "Yeah, babe."

Olivia: "I want so badly to make love to you right now. I'm still sore from the last time. Can you make very slow love to me and be very gentle with me? I may need a lot of lubrication this time, and I'm assuming that we don't have any here, but I'm willing to try to take you in."

Me: "Yes, of course, babe. I will never turn down the chance to make love to you."

We made slow, beautiful love. She was so overwhelmed over getting engaged, that as we were talking while making love, I could hear her pouting out the words. We could not stop kissing each other, and even though my cock was inside her, she never let on that it hurt or that I was too deep. Making love to my beautiful fiancé` was the most beautiful feeling that I had ever experienced.

Olivia: "I love you with all my heart and soul, baby. This is by far the best day of my life, even better than the day I met you. I cannot wait to be your wife. I'm going to cry again, I'm sorry."

Me: "Honey, we don't have to do this right now."

Olivia: "Yes, we do, baby. Don't you dare pull your cock out. I need to feel that this moment is real."

Me: "Olivia Jordanov, I love you more than you have ever dreamt that you could be loved. I will tell you each and every day for the rest of your life, how beautiful, how sexy, and how amazing you are. I promise you that."

Olivia: "Get your fiancé` pregnant, baby. Give us our baby girl. I want to feel you cum inside me. I want to feel you do that every day for the rest of my life."

Within a few minutes, she did feel me cum inside her and pulled me in closer to her so I couldn't pull out. We kept making love and kissing through the whole thing. If she was sore, she sure wasn't showing it right now. She rolled me over on my back and got on top of me. She put my cock back inside her and started riding me very fast until she was ready to squirt. When she was ready, she leaned up and squirted all over my chest. She was exhausted at this point, so she rolled over on her back, panting and moaning for a bit. I laid on my side and rubbed my hand over her belly and her breasts.

Olivia: "Mrs. Olivia Castle; I love the sound of that. This must be what heaven feels like."

After a few more minutes of intense kissing, we rolled out of bed and headed downstairs to sit at the dining room table so we could have a smoke and a glass of wine. We were still nude and did not think anything of it.

Olivia: "I still can't believe that this is our house. Sweetheart, I can already feel the magnetism of this house tingling through my body."

Me: “Well, this it. This is where we were destined to be, honey. This is the house that I saw in my dreams. And you are the lady of this beautiful house. We will have such a wonderful life here together. There is nothing but true, deep love within these walls and we’ve been very blessed with it.”

Olivia: “Honey, I’m going to be the best wife you have ever imagined, you’ll see.”

Me: “You already are, baby. You are the center of my world.”

Olivia: “Honey, I just want you to know that now that we are engaged to be married, I’m not expecting us to get married anytime soon. So, please don’t feel like I’m expecting that. Ok? And please don’t think that I want a huge wedding, because I don’t. Just you, me, my maid of honor, and your best man is all we need. Can we keep it that simple?”

Me: “Of course we can. I like to keep things simple.”

Olivia: “I would love to get married right here in this house. Is that ok with you?”

Me: “You read my mind, girl.”

Olivia could not take her eyes off her engagement ring. We had one more glass of wine and then headed back to the other house. We are going to make a very slow transition over to this new place. It was the end of the evening, and Olivia and I were looking forward to getting a good night's rest. After all she had been through today, she could definitely use it. She came to bed in her usual white T-shirt with no bra and no panties. She was constantly touching her engagement ring and kissing it. I’m sure she can’t wait to see how it sparkles when the sunlight hits it.

Olivia: "***Hmm!*** Wait a minute."

Me: "What?"

Olivia: "I just thought of something. Our new house is fucking huge. It's going to take me forever to clean it, so I think a big raise should be in order here." We both laughed.

Me: "Hun, just do the basics, and I will have a cleaning crew come in every month to give it a thorough cleaning. I've already thought about that."

Olivia: "I would be worried that they would go through our personal belongings. I'm not saying it's going to happen, but it could."

Me: "There are several cameras hidden throughout the whole place. I've got that covered."

We finally did fall asleep, and actually slept in quite a bit. It was a lazy day for both of us, and we needed to have a day where we did absolutely nothing. There is a local car show this weekend, and I was going to ask Olivia if she wanted to drive the Z/28, while I drove the Trans Am. I'm sure she'd be more than happy to drive it. She loved the beautiful red color, and how the color of the rims matched the body. The rims were off an old '78 Z/28 that I had.

Olivia did have a few errands to run really quick, so I just relaxed on the sofa. She was gone for a couple of hours. When she got home, I was sleeping on the sofa with music playing in the background. She walked over and kissed me on the forehead, and I woke up. She was holding a small, gift-wrapped bag behind her back. She was smiling from ear to ear.

Me: “Hi, Lover."

Olivia: “Hello, my sexy, handsome man. I have to ask you something. And whatever your response is, please know that I won’t be upset. Ok?”

Me: “Sure, what is it?"

Olivia: “How would you feel about wearing a wedding band on your ring finger even though we are not married, and even though we won't be for a while? Is that something you would entertain? I'm just wondering, that's all."

Me: “Sure, I would love to wear a wedding band on my finger.”

Olivia: “Good, because ***this*** is for you."

She reached her hand in the bag and handed me a little box, which obviously had a ring in it. I opened it up and it was a beautiful platinum wedding band. It was stunning and I was very proud to wear it for her. I don’t wear necklaces, but I do love wearing rings, especially this one.

Olivia: “Honey, please don't feel like you have to wear it just to please me."

Me: “Don’t be silly, I love wearing rings. I just don’t have many of them anymore.”

She put the ring on my finger, and we embraced in one of our infamous five-minute kisses. She had just made my day even more beautiful than it already was.

Olivia: “I can't wait to walk hand in hand with you as your fiancé'. Nothing makes me prouder than walking with the man of my dreams, holding his hand."

Me: "While I'm thinking of it, babe, there's a local car show this weekend, and I figured we could take the cars. What do you think?"

Olivia: "I would ***love*** that. Now I am very excited! ***I can't wait!*** "

Me: "It will be the last one of the Summer. The Fall season is right around the corner."

Olivia: "Yeah, I have noticed the nights cooling down lately. I don't mind the cooler weather, but when it gets below forty degrees I just want to hide inside all Winter. But on the other hand, now I have my sexy man to keep me warm."

The weekend was now here, and we were cleaning up the cars for the show. She just loved that red Z/28 and was happy to wash and wax it. We had our lunch, and we were ready to hit the car show. I told her to just be careful and follow me. She fired the Z/28 up, I fired up the Trans Am, and we were off. It was a twenty-minute drive once we hit the expressway. I can just imagine how many looks she was going to get driving that car. It was something to see.

We got there and put our cars in the lineup. Of course, guys were checking out the hottie in the red Z/28. She attracted a lot of attention. Olivia wore that red and black checkered shirt I got her, along with her cut off jean shorts, and those sexy work boots. We parked the cars, popped the hoods, and walked around the place holding hands and watching our rings sparkle in the sun. We were a very proud couple. After we walked around for a bit, we sat by our cars and talked to people, answering any questions they had about the cars. Several of my friends popped by and shot the shit with us for a while.

We met a lot of people at the car show. We were just loving it, being out there together, being in love, and recently engaged. I introduced her as my wife because that's what she really is to me, and she introduced me as her husband. That just made her eyes sparkle. I saw a few people there whom I had built homes for. We stayed for five or six hours and then decided to leave. From there we headed home to tuck the cars away in the garage, got in her Blazer, and drove over to the new house. I had a little bit of framing left to do in the garage and she already had on her sexy carpenter's outfit, so we put in a couple hours' worth of work, and then headed home.

It was getting late, and we were both exhausted, so we called it a night. We didn't make love because we were both on the tired side. Olivia mentioned that she wanted to get her nose and clit pierced, so the next morning after we had breakfast, I called my friend Shana, and she had an opening that afternoon. So, we went, and Olivia got her piercings. She looked extremely sexy with a gold hoop on one of her nostrils and another gold hoop on her sexy, shaved clit.

Olivia: "Do you like them baby? Do they look ok?"

Me: "They look very sexy on you. You wear them very well. As if you aren't sexy enough as it is."

With the weather getting colder now, she wouldn't be laying out in the sun anymore, but I'm sure she'll be walking around the house with next to nothing on as she always did. I did love seeing her wear that sexy maid's outfit as she was cleaning. A lot of times she still had it on when I got home from work, and I found that very enticing. She knew damn well how to get my juices flowing, and she also knew that once she bent over in front of me with that outfit on, it would only be a minute or so before I had my hands all over her entire body. Whatever room she teased me in was the room that we ended up making love in. We have had sex all over this house, many times, especially in the laundry room.

I remember one time; the postman was knocking on the door because I had to sign for a package. Olivia and I were in the middle of making love on the pullout sofa. As soon as he walked up the steps onto the deck, he heard Olivia moaning loud and clear. We didn't really want to stop, but we did. I was a little embarrassed to answer the door, while Olivia was embarrassed because the guy heard her squealing. If he was going to listen to us have sex, then we made sure he got a good earful.

Olivia: "Honey, when are you going to get me pregnant? I want a baby, sweetheart."

Me: "I know you do, babe, I'm trying. I'll make another deposit tonight." She chuckled.

Olivia: "Well, honey you'll have to settle for some mouth because I just got my period, which is surprising, considering how much we've had sex, and you've never pulled out."

Me: "You look upset that you're not pregnant."

Olivia: "I am not upset babe, not at all. I have often wondered if I could even have children. If I can't, then so be it."

Me: "I want children one day, but ***just*** for that one day." She laughed.

Olivia: "This has been the best year of my life. It was like we found each other at the exact time we were supposed to and saved each other. Well, I don't know if I saved ***you***, but you certainly saved ***me***, baby. I am living a completely different life now, than I was before I met you."

Me: "Whether you had been working at that hotel or not, I feel in my heart of hearts that we would have eventually found each other."

Things did happen rather fast for us, and sometimes you can't leave things to chance. I could have chosen any number of hotels in that area, but me choosing the one that she worked at was obviously fate. They say things happen for a reason, for whatever reason, good or bad. Soon we will start moving into our new home. We may wait until after the first of the year.

It was the very next morning, and after she made us a beautiful breakfast, she wanted to go grocery shopping, so we went together. We both found it very romantic to be walking hand in hand out in public. We absolutely loved being in love. We weren't the type to be making out in front of people. We saved all of that for the bedroom. After we got home from shopping, we decided to take a walk and get some fresh air. Nature is so beautiful to look at, we both enjoyed it. I brought my camera with me and took dozens of pictures of old farmhouses and tractors. Of course, I had to take several pictures of Olivia sporting her engagement ring.

Olivia: "Honey, are we doing anything for Thanksgiving? I mean, do you usually go to your parents' house to celebrate the holidays?"

Me: "My family is completely dysfunctional. We were never close, so I tend to stay home for the holidays."

Olivia: "Yeah, I can relate to that, honey. Don't get me wrong, my parents and I love each other very deeply, but it was just time that I went out on my own and tried to be independent. I obviously left home too soon. I got impatient, I guess. This will be our first Thanksgiving together and I want to make it a very special one for you."

Me: "Well, honey, you're in luck because you love to cook, and I love to eat, so I guess we already have something special."

Olivia: "***Smart Ass!*** I love the holiday season. I love the snow covering the trees and bushes, it is so beautiful. All the Christmas lights on peoples' houses and windows as they sparkle off the snow, it is so nice to see. I also love it when people have large figurines covered in lights on their lawns."

Me: "Well, honey, it doesn't snow around here too often. Sometimes we do luck out and get snow falling on Christmas morning, but not very often. Why do you think that I don't own any snowmobiles? I would buy one, but then I would have to transport it just to ride it."

Olivia: "Do you decorate the house at all with lights?"

Me: "I haven't up to this point, but with you here we'll make it a tradition. Sound good?"

Olivia: "I would love that, baby. I may even have a special Christmas outfit tucked away just for you."

Me: "Honey, it doesn't matter what you wear, you're going to look absolutely beautiful."

Olivia: "These are going to be the best holidays ever. I want to make them so special for you, and for ***us***. I feel like I've already gotten the best Christmas gift ever; this beautiful diamond ring from the man of my dreams."

Me: "Olivia, I have never been excited about the holidays. But now I can't help but feel so happy, so blessed, and so loved. I really do feel like I am living my dream with the most beautiful lady I had ***ever*** imagined. I just ***knew*** you were out there, waiting to come into my life."

Olivia: "Honey, let's make a promise right now that we will ***never*** go to bed mad at each other, ***ever!*** Our love is way beyond that, and I know we're both mature and responsible enough to talk about anything that may be bothering us. Please, honey, let's promise each other, right now."

Me: "I promise you, honey. I would never try to intentionally upset you or make you cry. I love you way too much to ever do that."

Olivia: "You just know how to melt my heart, sweetheart. Love really does make a home so much happier."

Chapter 7 – Fall Is Upon Us

With the Fall weather creeping up on us, it was time to think about going into hibernation mode for the next five or six months. I couldn't hunker down during these months because I still had houses to build, but my sweet Olivia was looking very forward to chilling for the Winter months. I had plenty of work for me and my crew well into Springtime of next year. We were in November now, and that usually means colder weather and lots of warm snuggle time with my beautiful fiancé`. Olivia and I went to a Halloween party last month at Eric's house. We had a blast that night and I also broadcasted that Olivia, and I were officially engaged to be married. Olivia dressed up as a sexy chambermaid, go figure, and I went as a carpenter. We basically wore our daily attire, just to someone else's house.

We haven't set a wedding date yet because we are in no hurry for a piece of paper. We live and love as man and wife already, so a wedding date is not a priority to us right now. Olivia was in her glory showing off her beautiful engagement ring, and of course I flaunted my stunning wedding band that she got for me. She has been glowing ever since we got engaged, and I feel like a different man all together, knowing that I will have Olivia's love for the rest of my life.

Olivia and I were on the deck on the two-person swing having a cup of coffee and a smoke, talking about the holiday season. We both knew that neither one of us was going to any relatives or sibling's house. She was a lot like me in that she liked to stay disconnected from the outside world. We were both extreme introverts and just loved being in our humble home together. Neither one of us really has the desire to converse with the outside world. I have to, because of my profession, but that's it.

Olivia: "Honey, have you given any thought as to what we should do for Thanksgiving? It will be our first one together and I want it to be perfect."

Me: "Actually babe, how do you feel about going out to a very prestigious restaurant for Thanksgiving dinner? It would save you from stressing about cooking all the food and being overwhelmed."

Olivia: "Actually, honey, that's a great idea. It's not like we have any family close by to share the day with. My parents live in a different state, and I have no siblings. And from what you've told me about your family, you don't get along too good."

Me: "Yeah, that's too bad, but it is what it is, right?"

Olivia: "Well, we have each other, baby, and that's all we need."

Me: "I'm assuming that you have a nice outfit to wear for our special turkey dinner. Or do we need to get you one?"

Olivia: "Baby, I have ***just the outfit*** for that special night."

Me: "Is it crotchless?" She laughed.

Olivia: "It is not crotchless, but I'm sure it will get your attention. When have I ***ever*** not dressed sexy for you, honey? It doesn't matter ***what*** I wear because when we get back home, you're only going to rip it off me before I get my foot in the door. And you know as well as I do that shortly after that, we're heading to bed to make love." She gives me a wink.

Olivia and I had sex all the time. Sometimes we did it three times a day, depending on how sore she was from the last time. I guess that's to be expected when two people are newly acquainted, and they can't seem to keep their hands off each other. Olivia and I are no exception. We act like a couple of high school kids that are experiencing love and sex for the first time.

Olivia: "Honey, do you remember that time when the postman came to the door, and we were fucking on the sofa as he was knocking on the door?"

Me: "I do, yes. Why do you ask?"

Olivia: "Because I saw him at the grocery store today. He has seen me laying out in the yard before when he was delivering our mail, so, I'm quite sure that he knew it was me getting laid. He looked at me kind of funny as he walked by. I wonder what he was thinking. I sort of felt embarrassed, but on the other hand, I'm pretty sure that him hearing us have sex brought some excitement to his day."

Me: "Did he say anything to you?"

Olivia: "No, but I made sure he got a good look at my ass as I walked by him."

Me: "I'm sure he wished that he was the one giving you dick instead of me."

Olivia: "My sweet Julian is the ***only man*** who will ***ever*** have his cock inside me. Speaking of that, baby, I got my period today. So, you'll have to settle for some mouth. Are you happy with my oral skills, honey? I've never done it before meeting you, so I really don't know what I'm doing. I will admit that I have been watching videos on how to properly give a blowjob." She blushed.

Me: "Honey, you're doing just fine in that department. And I'm not just saying that."

We were both getting tired, so we headed off to bed. I was going to work in the morning and putting in a very long day. Once Olivia and I move over to our new house, I'm going to turn one of the spare rooms into an office area, and Olivia will be handling all the work-related phone calls and any other concerns about current and future home builds. So, she's not only my sexy maid and fiancé`, but she's also going to be my hot office secretary. She really is looking forward to being directly involved in the business end of my profession. She can navigate a computer way better than me and seems to have decent people skills.

Olivia: "Honey, I have to ask you something. I got ahold of an old high school friend on the internet. She was actually my only friend in high school, and when we graduated, we lost touch because she moved away. Anyways, she's been out this way seeing her parents, and I wondered how you might feel about having her over for Thanksgiving, if she can make it. Her name is Vivian, and she has always been the only girl I could talk to who could relate to me."

Me: "That's fine, babe. When will she be heading this way?"

Olivia: "Well, she's at her parent's house right now, and I was going to see if she could spend a day or two here with us. How do you feel about that? Are you ok with that? I have missed her so much through the years."

Me: "I'm ok with that. Whatever you want, honey. She's not a psycho, is she? Am I going to have to lock up my guns?" She laughed.

Olivia: "No, baby, I can assure you of that. I've missed her so much. We used to hang out every day after school. She and I always felt like outcasts in school, so that's what brought us together. She was my one true friend, as I was hers."

Me: "Honey, I think it would be great for you to see your best friend again. So, with her coming over for Thanksgiving, did you still want to go out for dinner, or stay home and cook?"

Olivia: "Let's stay home, baby. She can help me with all the cooking and preparation."

Me: "If that's what you want, then that sounds like a plan."

Olivia: "I will reach out to her shortly and see if she can make it here. Thank you so much for this, honey. Just promise me one thing, ok?"

Me: "Sure, what is it?"

Olivia: "Vivian was quite the hot looking young lady in school, so if she still looks like that, please promise me that you won't take an intimate interest in her. She is very flirtatious with a hot ass body, that's how I remember her looking."

Me: "Well, you have nothing to worry about. I happen to be engaged to sexiest, most beautiful lady on this planet, and ***no one*** comes close to her."

Olivia: "Really? Do I know her?" She chuckled.

Olivia did get ahold of Vivian, and as it turns out, she will be joining us for Thanksgiving. Olivia is all excited about it, and I love to see her happy and smiling. Thanksgiving wasn't for another two weeks, but I think Vivian might be coming here very soon, as in, within the next few days.

Olivia: "Honey, Vivian will be here by Friday afternoon, if that's ok."

Me: "Of course it is. I'm looking forward to meeting her. We'll show her a good time while she's here."

Olivia: "Thanks again, baby. This means so much to me."

It was Friday now, and I was at work when Olivia sent me a text telling me that Vivian had arrived. She was ecstatic, and I was happy for her. I still had a couple of hours' worth of work to do before I was going to leave. I think it was around 6:30 p.m. when I got home, and Olivia and Vivian were sitting at the table having some wine and a smoke. When I walked into the house, they both stood up and this is what I saw of Vivian. She was about 5′ 6″ tall, like Olivia, athletic body, long, wavy, auburn colored hair, almost red, and the brightest blue eyes I had ever seen in my life. They were very inviting, but also very intimidating, very piercing. Olivia did tell me that she was a genuine redhead, even though her hair was a lot darker now. As far as her breasts were concerned, they were the same size as Olivia's; just perfect. She had one of her nostrils pierced just like Olivia, and it looked very nice on her. She smelled very nice and seemed very easy to talk to. Olivia wasn't kidding, Vivian was quite hot and sexy looking.

Olivia: "Honey, this is Vivian, and Vivian, this is my fiancé`, Julian."

Vivian: "Well, hello, Julian. It's a pleasure to meet you. I've gotten quite the earful about you since I've been here. Thank you for making my best friend so happy. I have never seen her like this before. It means a lot to me to see her smiling."

Me: "It's a pleasure to meet you, Vivian. Welcome, and make yourself at home."

Vivian: "Olivia did tell me that you were a very sexy and handsome man, and she wasn't kidding about that. Do you have a twin brother or sister by any chance?" We laughed.

Olivia: "Easy, girl, this one's not for the taking. He's all mine. Aren't you, baby?"

Me: "I'm very proud to say that I am. I do find it very ironic though, that two of the most beautiful women I have ever seen in my life were labelled outcasts in high school. You ***had*** to have had guys all over you."

Vivian: "We didn't waste our time with immature boys in high school. I'm willing to bet that most of them ***still*** haven't matured yet."

Olivia: "We weren't part of any clicks, and we certainly didn't play any sports."

Vivian: "Well, we ***did*** get high a few times before school, so maybe that classified us as stoners. Whatever the case, most of the other students annoyed us, so we chose to keep our distance from them. I'm sure we were seen as being very weird to them. Who cares, right?"

Me: "Honey, I'm going to hop in the shower really quick. I'll be back in a few. Enjoy your wine, ladies."

As I was showering, Vivian and Olivia continued to catch up on life, while finishing off a bottle of wine, and listening to some music. Vivian did say that she could stay through Thanksgiving weekend but had to head back home after that.

Vivian: "You seem very happy and content here. This is a nice place you have, looks very peaceful and quiet. What else would you expect from living out in the country, right?"

Olivia: "He actually just finished building us a house up over the hill. He started building it long before he met me. That's where we got engaged, in the new place. I will tell you all about it. The place is fucking huge and gorgeous. ***It is stunning!*** "

Vivian: "I'm jealous. But I'm very happy for you. He seems like a very decent, hardworking man. I wish I could find one like him. The men I've dated recently are only looking for one thing, and I'm so done with that. I can't seem to find someone who's trustworthy and committed."

Olivia: "Well, I was a virgin when we met and that didn't scare him away at all."

Vivian: "***What? You were still a virgin, girl?"***

Olivia: "***Yep!*** We didn't have sex until we were together for at least five months. That's how it worked out for us. Originally, he hired me to be his maid, but soon after I moved in, we started to flirt with each other, and it just escalated from there. Almost six months later I had sex for the very first time, ever. And two months after that, we were engaged."

Vivian: "That's the sort of thing you read about in fairy tales. Good for you, Olivia. I can tell by the way he looks at you that he really loves you and vice versa. I would love to find a real man like him. I've pretty much given up on that. Lately I've preferred dating women anyways, to be honest."

Olivia: "You'll find the right one, girl. Give it time."

Vivian: "How is the sex? Do you find yourselves having sex all the time now?"

Olivia: "It's amazing. Yes, we've had sex all over this house, even in the new house, the night we got engaged."

Vivian: "I envy how much you two have sex. Am I going to hear you moaning tonight while I'm trying to get some sleep?" Olivia chuckled.

Olivia: "We'll try to resist ourselves since we have company over, but I can't promise you that."

Vivian: "How is his package? Is he big? It sure looks big, not that I was trying to notice."

Olivia: "Oh, he is plenty big, girl. It feels like he's splitting me in half; I can tell you that much."

We were all drinking wine and feeling fine. We had some snacks to eat. I suggested ordering pizza and wings. They were all for that idea. I placed the order, and within thirty-five minutes I was off to get the food.

Olivia: "So, are you seeing anyone right now? Any man in your life?"

Vivian: "Not really. I do date this one guy, but we don't see each other too often, unless one of us needs to get laid. Like I said, I'm leaning more towards dating women these days."

Olivia: "Haven't had sex in a while, huh?"

Vivian: "No, about four or five months, I guess. That's why I have my dildos." She chuckled.

Olivia: "I don't own any sex toys, and he hasn't asked me to use any either. I would though if he asked, probably. I get enough from him, more than enough."

Vivian: "Is he good in bed? Not that you've had anyone to compare him to."

Olivia: "He is an amazing lover. Right after he popped my cherry it seems like all we do is have sex. It's going to take me a while to get used to it, I'm sure. I don't know if it's because he's so big or because I'm so tight."

Vivian: "That's good; a man who really knows how to fuck."

Olivia: "Yeah, and he never pulls out, even our first time, he came inside me. He told me that he loved me enough already to get me pregnant with no regrets. So now I ***won't*** let him pull out."

Vivian: "You must really love him to let him cum in you all the time. If that were me, I'd probably be pregnant by now."

Olivia: "We were in love already by the first time we made love, so no, I don't want him to ever pull out. Before we actually had sex there was a lot of oral sex. I'm still learning how to properly suck his dick. I'm not very good at it yet. Why am I telling you this? I'm so embarrassed."

Vivian: "Don't be, this is ***me*** you're talking to. Whatever we've always talked about is sacred to me. You should know that by now."

Olivia: "I know, I trust you. And whatever you tell me never leaves my mouth. You really are the one and only true friend that I have."

I arrived with the food and couldn't wait to eat. I was so glad Olivia and Vivian were having a great time. Vivian changed into something more comfortable. She did have quite the body, like Olivia, and also sported an ultra-fine ass.

Olivia: "Honey, is it possible at all to get in the hot tub? I know you've covered it up for the season, but would it be a lot of work to fire it up again?"

Me: "No problem at all, just give me a few minutes."

Olivia: "Vivian, do you want to soak in the hot tub?"

Vivian: "You don't have to ask me twice, sister, let's do it."

I took the cover off the hot tub, added a little more water to it, and then fired it up. They both only had on white T-shirts and panties. And I noticed that Vivian took off her bra. I could clearly see Vivian's "*pooter*" through her panties. I wanted to see if she shaved her crotch like my sweet Olivia did. She had tattoos all over her thighs. A couple of them extended around to her lower back and ass.

Vivian: "This is awesome, girl. It feels so refreshing on my body. It's been a long time since I've been in one of these."

Olivia: "Yeah, we love it. I'm so glad the new place has one too. I can't wait to move in there. It is stunning, Vivian. He is such a great carpenter, a great guitar player, a great lover, and a great man. I am so deeply in love with him."

Vivian: "I can tell that you are. You are glowing, and it makes me happy to see you happy. Is he selling this place when you move into the new one?"

Olivia: "He is not sure yet. Why? Do you want to buy it?"

Vivian: "I wish I could call a place my own. I'm not there yet obviously. One day though. So, I need to find a guy like your Julian to take care of me and love me unconditionally."

Olivia: "Give it time, girl. You'll find the right man when you're not looking for him. I met him completely out of the blue and unexpectedly. It was the best day of my life. I've never looked back, and he genuinely treats me like a lady, not just his maid or a piece of ass."

Vivian: "Have you two fucked in this hot tub yet?"

Olivia: "No, not yet. We came close a few times though."

I walked out onto the deck to check up on them. They were having a wonderful time, and I was glad for them. It was all about seeing my sweet Olivia smile, and she was, from ear to ear.

Vivian: "You're not getting in, Julian?"

Me: "No. You two have fun with it. This is your girl talk time."

Olivia: "Come on in honey and sit next to your lady."

Vivian: "The lady of the house has spoken, so now you have to get in with us, that's the rule."

Me: "Why do you ladies even have those T-shirts on? I can see right through them."

Olivia: "He's right, you know. We're all friends here. I'll keep my panties on though, not that it would matter. I'm sure my panties are see-through, just like the shirt was."

Vivian left her panties on too. She had a tattoo just below her belly button. It was a gorgeous green vine with red roses and thorns hanging off it. It definitely drew attention to her crotch area. It was very finely detailed and looked amazing. I had a hard time keeping my eyes off her tattoos. She was very easy to talk to and had a great sense of humor. Olivia just adored having her here. As I looked at Vivian, I did wonder how many men have had the privilege of getting between her legs, not that I wanted to, because I didn't. She was definitely gorgeous and sexy enough that she could have any man she wanted; married, or single. At least that's my opinion of her.

Olivia: "Vivian, maybe tomorrow we'll take you up and show you the new house if you want to see it. I love being in this house because we have a lot of precious memories already."

Vivian: "I would love to see it. This place right here is very nice and cozy. The new place must be something special if you're willing to leave this one."

Me: "I started building it earlier last year, in between all of my other jobs. I wasn't in a hurry to finish it, but soon after I met Olivia, my calling was to finish it, because I felt we had something very special. She is my driving force."

Olivia: "Oh honey, your words are so touching to me."

Vivian: "You two have something very special here, and I wish both of you a lifetime of happiness together. I mean that."

Me: "Hey Vivian, if you ever want to move out this way, and need a place to stay, let me know and I may be able to set you up here."

Vivian: "Really? I will have to think about that, and thank you so much for the offer, Julian. To be honest, I would love to move away to some place that's in the middle of nowhere. I am so sick of the city life, all the crime and drama, and most people are phonies and rude."

Me: "I'm just leaving it as an option for you in the future, providing I don't sell this place. But we'd love to have you as our neighbor, and I'd rather sell the house to someone I know."

The ladies were getting quite tipsy from the wine, and it was time to get them out of the hot tub. They had one more smoke as they were finishing their wine and decided to get out. I handed them both towels, and we all went inside. Olivia changed into her short, silky robe, and Vivian did the same thing. The robes barely covered their asses. They obviously didn't care, and neither did I.

Olivia: "I'm tired from the wine. I think I'm going to call it a night, folks. This wine is kicking my butt, and I will probably have a headache in the morning."

She kissed me good night, hugged Vivian, and then she was off to bed. I decided to go into my music room and mix down some tracks with the headphones on so that I wouldn't wake Olivia. I was trying to be as quiet as I could.

Me: "Vivian, help yourself to everything, and if you need something, I'll be right down the hall in my music room."

Vivian: "Thank you, Julian. Are you going to play guitar now?"

Me: "No, it will wake Olivia, so tonight I'm just going to mix down some guitar tracks. I will have my headphones on."

Vivian: "Ok. I'll see you in the morning. Thanks again for having me here, Julian. It means a lot to Olivia and me that we re-connected after all this time."

Me: "See you in the morning. Good night." We hugged.

Vivian chilled on the sofa bed and tried to find a good movie to watch. About two hours had passed when I came out of the music room and heard the TV on, so I went out into the living room and Vivian was sleeping. I reached over and turned off the TV. She was laying on her side facing away from me, and her robe wasn't covering up her ass, so I did get a good look at it. I grabbed the blanket off the back of the couch and laid it over her. She felt me do that, and then rolled over on her back. She looked up at me really quick, and I made sure she was covered up. She dozed back off into dreamland, and I decided to get some rest myself.

The next morning when I got up, the ladies were already sitting at the table having coffee and a smoke. I didn't realize that I had slept in; I usually don't. I was always up before Olivia. I walked over to the table and gave Olivia a good morning kiss.

Olivia: "Good morning, baby, I love you."

Me: "Morning honey, I love you. Good morning, Vivian."

Vivian: "Good morning, Julian."

Me: "What time did you two get up?"

Olivia: "About two hours ago. You must have really been tired honey because you never sleep this late."

Me: "Yeah, I know. It's already 10:00 a.m."

Olivia: "Vivian and I are going to go shopping after we hit the shower. So, if there's anything you need honey, let me know."

Me: "Honey will you scratch my back really quick, please?"

Olivia: "Sure, baby."

I stood up in front of where she was sitting, lifted my shirt, and she scratched my back. A minute later I walked over and grabbed a cup of coffee and sat with them. I was sitting across from Vivian, and she looked at me with those piercing blue eyes. I wondered if they glowed in the dark; that's how bright they are. She reminded me of a groupie from the 1980's when I was playing out all the time. Her hair was so long and wavy, and it had a very sexy red color to it. The one thing that I loved about the 1980's was all the beautiful women with huge hair. That was the thing back then, and to this day, I still favor those sexy hair styles.

Me: "So Vivian, did you enjoy your first night here? Did you two ladies have fun?"

Olivia: "I remembered the hot tub feeling amazing on my body, and then the wine kicked in."

Vivian: "I did, it was great. The hot tub was amazing. We drank a lot of wine, I remember that. And I remember watching a movie, and then sometime during the night I remember you putting a blanket over me."

Me: "Well, when I finished up in the music room, I heard the TV on. I walked out and saw you sleeping on the sofa bed with no covers. Your robe was barely on you so I figured you might be cold. It can get quite cool in here at night."

Vivian: "Thank you for doing that for me. Was I completely naked?"

Me: "Just about."

Olivia: "Did you check out her pooter, baby?"

Vivian: "My pooter?"

Olivia: "That's what he calls our pussies, just so you know."

Vivian: "I was born in Georgia, so I've always referred to mine as a "peach". Ok, if you saw my peach, then what color is my clit ring?"

Olivia: "I hope you don't know the answer to that, baby." She chuckled.

Vivian: "I'm sure it's nothing he hasn't seen before."

Me: "I don't know, I didn't see it. It was covered up by your robe. I'm not a pervert so I didn't try to see it. I did get a great look at your ass though. You and Olivia both have ultra-fine asses."

Olivia: "I find it very hard to believe that you haven't been laid in four or five months. I mean, look at you, girl. You're very pretty with a body to die for."

Me: "Four or five months? You're kidding, right? Not to sound like a pervert, but if you were my girl, I would be all over you, Vivian. I can't keep my hands off Olivia. You don't strike me as the type of lady who has any trouble at all getting a man."

Vivian: "I've had my fair share, trust me. It just seems like everyone wants to get laid, but no one wants commitment. I don't want to do that anymore. I want to fall in love and have someone fall in love with me as well. At least if I keep dating women, then there's a less chance of me getting my heart broken. I'm so done with the whole dating bull shit. Even when I do have sex these days, I don't get pure joy out of it because I know it doesn't mean anything to the person I'm sleeping with. It's just casual sex."

Olivia: "Aww, girl, don't give up on love just because you came across a few bad seeds. I was in the dumps too before I met Julian. And now look at us."

Vivian: "I ***am*** looking at both of you. I want what you two have. I'm beginning to think that I'm just not worthy of finding true, deep love. I'm honestly considering a life a celibacy. Maybe I really do need to find out who I really am, and what I really need. I mean, I don't ***need*** a man in my life. I have plenty of toys to get me off when I need to." We laughed.

Me: "Olivia and me ***both*** have toys; I kid you not."

Vivian: "Umm, ***what?*** "

Olivia: "Yeah, honey, ***what?*** "

Me: "They're in the garage. Hers is red and mine is black."

Olivia: "Oh, he's talking about the cars, girl. You ***have*** to see his cars, they're gorgeous."

Vivian: "I would love to see them. What are they?"

Me: "1981 Camaro Z/28 and 1977 Pontiac Trans Am."

Vivian: "I ***love*** the older cars. Now I ***have*** to see them. Show me, please."

After we had our breakfast, Olivia and I took Vivian out to the garage to see the cars. She was very impressed with them and appreciated the older vehicles.

Vivian: "That Trans Am is fucking sexy, Julian. I would gladly spread my legs on ***that*** hood. That Z/28 is stunning too. You have great taste in cars. I'll have to come back in the Spring so you can take me for a ride in them."

Olivia: "I love driving the Z/28. The Trans Am, however, scares the ***shit*** out of me."

Vivian: "Oh, I would ***love*** to drive that car. I can drive a manual, no problem. Something that sexy would definitely make me squirt in my shorts. Did I say that out loud?" She chuckled.

Olivia: "You are such a whore, girl." They laughed.

Vivian: "I'm not a whore in real life, but I do play one on TV."

Me: "Really? What porn movies have you played in?" We laughed.

Vivian: "Oh, you're really funny, ***honey!*** "

We went back inside, and the ladies tried to come up with a list of things that we're going to need for Thanksgiving dinner. We pondered the thought of still going out for Thanksgiving dinner. Olivia loves to cook, so making a big dinner would be nothing for her. I wasn't expecting a huge dinner anyways, and I don't even eat turkey on Thanksgiving. I prefer ham, myself, and I love homemade mashed potatoes with stuffing and corn. Thanksgiving wasn't until next week, so we had plenty of time to prepare for it.

Me: "Hey, let's take a ride out to the new place so Vivian can see it. Does that sound good?"

Vivian: "I would love to see it. Olivia said you worked very hard on the house and she's proud of you and impressed with your carpentry skills."

Olivia: "He's a great builder, I envy his talent."

Me: "She's just saying that to be nice. I don't have any real skills that I'm aware of."

Olivia: "He's lying. He ***knows*** he's quite talented. Honey, can we take the Z/28 up to the new house? ***Pretty please, baby?*** "

Me: "Sure, you can. You can drive and Vivian can ride with you. I'll take the Trans Am."

Vivian: "Olivia, you're on your own girl, ***I'm*** riding in the Trans Am with ***him***."

Olivia: "Ok. I'm just excited to drive it again."

I grabbed the keys to the cars from the house and we were off to the new place. Olivia was leading the way, and as I was shifting the Trans Am into gear, Vivian puts her hand over mine and held it there.

Vivian: "You don't mind, do you? It makes me feel like I'm driving it."

Me: "No, you're fine. By the way, you smell very nice."

Vivian: "Thank you. Olivia sprayed it on me. I ***love*** the smell. It's my new favorite perfume."

Me: "You really love this car, don't you?"

Vivian: "Oh yeah, I do. I would get very horny driving this car."

Me: "Don't start squirting all over my seats."

Vivian: "Trust me, honey, if I start squirting it's going to hit the windshield. You'd need windshield wipers on the inside of the car too. I have an ultra-moist peach." She winks.

Me: "Are you aware of what you say sometimes? Are you always this horny?"

Vivian: "No, I'm just very comfortable being around you and Olivia. To some guy I may just be a piece of ass, but when I'm around you two I feel respected, cared for and loved, if that makes any sense."

Me: "I understand what you're saying, and yes, we respect you. I know that Olivia adores you."

We pulled up to the house and Vivian was beside herself. Olivia still got goose bumps looking at it, and to be honest, when I looked at it myself, I got this overwhelming feeling of pride. We got out of the cars and walked around the place looking at the yard, the pool, and all of the beautiful black steel fencing surrounding the yard. Olivia and Vivian still couldn't believe their eyes. It was a proud moment.

Vivian: "Julian, this is beautiful. You built this?"

Me: "I did, with a lot of help. My sweet Olivia even put on her tool belt and helped me out."

Olivia: "Oh honey, this is just beyond words for me. I love you so much."

Me: "I love you too, honey. Let's go inside."

We walked inside, and we were all just floored by its beauty. It was a new chapter in our lives and all the craftsmanship that went into this house was top notch. My friends went above and beyond when they helped me build this. I couldn't thank them enough.

Vivian: "***Wow!*** This is amazing. I love the chandeliers and huge windows. The words for it are way beyond my vocabulary. It's very stunning, to say the least."

Olivia: "Come here Viv, I want to show you the kitchen. It has all stainless-steel appliances that I personally picked out."

They walked into the kitchen and saw all of the marble countertops, ceramic flooring, and stainless appliances. Olivia started to cry a little.

Vivian: "What's wrong, girl?"

Olivia: "This is where he proposed to me and gave me the ring. I'm sorry, I don't mean to cry. He just makes me so happy, Vivian. I love that man with all my heart and soul."

Vivian: "You have a lot to be thankful for. You deserve it. You deserve each other." She hugged Olivia.

Me: "Show her the whole place, honey. Show her how you had the bedrooms laid out, and the bathrooms too. You have a lot to be proud of. These furnishings were all your idea."

Vivian: "You picked out all the interior furnishings?"

Olivia: "Yeah, that was me. He let me have full reign of all those decisions. I didn't know, as I was ordering them, that they were actually going to be for ***our own house.*** "

Vivian: "You have great taste, girl. That's quite the hidden talent you possess. That staircase with the glass railings is fucking beautiful. I can see a lot of thought and hard work went into this place. Julian, you are very talented, that's admirable."

Olivia: "I'm just so happy, happier than I've ever been in my life, and I don't know how to deal with these beautiful emotions. I'm so proud to love him and so honored to be loved by him."

Vivian: "These are beautiful feelings you're experiencing, and you need to enjoy them to the fullest."

Olivia: "I'm so glad to have you as my best friend. You and Julian mean the world to me. I feel very blessed. I love you both so much."

Vivian: "Girl, you have a very nice life here, and hopefully if things work out, I'll be around to enjoy it with you. Do you think I'm going to let you enjoy that pool and hot tub ***by yourself?*** "

Olivia: "There's a king size bed in every bedroom, four huge bedrooms. Every bedroom has a huge walk-in closet. The master bedroom has its own bathroom in addition to the one in the hall. ***It's insane!*** "

Vivian: "I think I want to live here with you two, instead of the other house." They both chuckled.

Olivia: "Well, knowing my sweet Julian, I'm sure he'd probably let you if you asked him."

Vivian: "I would never ask him for that. This is your place for you and your future husband to enjoy for the rest of your lives. Which one is the master bedroom, the one you'll be sleeping in?"

Olivia: "Come here, I'll show you. They're all big enough to be master bedrooms."

Olivia showed Vivian the master bedroom as well as the other bedrooms. She was very impressed and shocked that the rooms were so big. She asked Olivia to call me upstairs for a minute.

Olivia: "Honey, can you come upstairs for a minute, please?"

I got to the top of the stairs and the ladies were standing in the hallway in front of the bedrooms.

Me: "What's up, honey?"

Vivian: "Olivia told me that you had sex in the master bedroom the night that you got engaged."

Me: "Umm, yes, we did. Why? Did you want to be here too?" They laughed.

Vivian: "I'm just wondering if you've also had sex in this room here, across from the master bedroom."

Me: "No, not yet. But I'm sure we'll christen the other three rooms very soon. Why do you ask? Are you going to record us?" We all laughed.

Vivian: "Well, is there any way you two could refrain from having sex on ***this bed***, at least until ***I've*** been laid on it, because I want this to be ***my*** bedroom."

Olivia: "I think we can bypass that one for the time being."

We finished showing Vivian our new house and headed back to the old one. Olivia was so excited that she got to drive the Z/28 again. Vivian, on the other hand, loved the Trans Am, so I let her drive it back home. It was a descent day out, so we took the cars for a short cruise. I was impressed with how good Vivian could drive. She was driving like a pro. When we got back home, they pulled the cars into the garage, where they were probably going to stay until Springtime.

It was a few days before Thanksgiving, and we decided to go out for dinner after all. Olivia took Vivian out to buy a nice outfit for the occasion. They said I couldn't see their outfits until we were ready to leave for dinner. That could only mean one thing: they're wearing something provocative and sexy. As if they weren't gorgeous and sexy enough, right? I'll just have to wait and see what they have in store for me. Knowing Olivia's taste in clothes, I'm sure they'll both be nothing short of breath-taking.

Olivia: "Honey, did you remember to call the restaurant for our reservations?"

Me: "I sure did. It's a good thing too, because the place is usually packed at all times."

Vivian: "I'm so glad I came here. Thank you so much for having me. I hope that I haven't been too much of a burden on you."

Olivia: "Don't be silly, girl. We love having you here. I'm a little sad that you have to leave in a few days. I do hope you consider staying in this house when we move to the other one for good."

Vivian: "I don't know, girl. It's a lot to think about. Don't get me wrong, I would love to be here, close to you. I'm just not someone who handles change very well. It scares me a little, to be honest."

Me: "Whenever you're ready, Vivian, ***if*** you're ready. I won't feel put out if you say no. All I know is that when Olivia first came here, she felt like a completely different person almost immediately."

Vivian: "I can understand why, Julian. I mean, she has an amazing man to share her life with, a man that worships the ground she walks on. I want ***that***. I want someone to look at me and never be able to take their eyes off of me."

Olivia: "Honey, it ***will*** happen for you. Give it time, girl. Any man worth his salt would absolutely die to be loved by you. You really are one very sexy, beautiful, and amazing lady. You have one hell of a knockout body too, girl."

Me: "She's right, Vivian. You really are all that, and then some. I don't mind telling you in front of my fiancé` that you are drop dead gorgeous. And it's not just your looks, it's your dynamic personality too. You seem to be very easy to talk to."

Vivian: "You know, you two are making it very hard for me to leave. I just want you to know that. I'm not looking forward to leaving, at all. I know I've only been here for a very short while, but I just had that feeling when I pulled in your driveway, that I'd never want to leave."

It was now Thanksgiving Day, and we were all getting ready to go out for dinner. It didn't take me long to get ready, so I just sat at the table waiting for the ladies to come out of the bedroom. All of a sudden, I heard the sound of high heels clicking on the hardwood floor. Out they came in these black and pink laced, long sleeved mini dresses, wearing the *"Angel"* perfume. Their hair was pulled back behind their ears. Describing how they looked does them absolutely no justice. They were dressed to impress.

Olivia: "How do we look, baby? Is this going to do it for you?"

Me: "***Oh, hell yes!*** You two are the most beautiful women I have ever seen. It's going to be very hard eating my meal while looking at the both of you."

Vivian: "Well, maybe you ought to hold off on getting ***hard*** until we get back home." She winked.

Me: "Vivian, you are a doll. You're so fucking adorable."

Olivia: "She sure is, honey. That's our sexy Vivian."

After we all had a smoke, we left for dinner. The restaurant was about forty-five minutes away from my house. We took Olivia's Blazer since it had the most room in it. Olivia was driving, and Vivian was in the front passenger seat. I was just chilling in the back seat, listening to the radio, and admiring how beautiful and sexy the ladies looked. I could smell their perfume clearly, and it was driving me insane. We arrived at the restaurant, and the valet parked the car. As we were walking towards the place, Olivia and I were holding hands, like we always did in public.

Vivian: "Umm, I'm feeling a little slighted here. Can I hold someone's hand?" She chuckled.

Me: "Sure, Sexy Red, I would be honored to hold your hand."

Olivia: "Awe, how romantic and cute."

As we were waiting to be seated, we sat at the bar and had a quick drink. I sat between them, and we just looked around at all the people there. I knew it wouldn't take long before the ladies started getting eye fucked by guys checking out the two hotties at the bar. It happened every time I took Olivia out in public, and with Vivian here, that just added more fuel to the fire. Olivia and I had wedding rings on, but Vivian did not, so the guys probably saw her as being single. After only a few minutes, this one guy walked over and sat next to Vivian.

Bar Guy: "Hello young lady, how are you? I'm Jeff, can I buy you a drink? I don't like to drink alone, and neither should you."

Vivian: "I'm all set, but thanks for asking."

Jeff: "What did you say your name was?"

Vivian: "I didn't, but nice try though. I don't want you to be under the impression that I'm here looking to hook up."

Jeff: "Who are you here with?"

Vivian: "I'm here with this handsome man, and his beautiful wife." We waved at him.

Jeff: "Well, where's ***your*** man? You shouldn't be alone on Thanksgiving."

Vivian: "This ***is*** my man. Honey, say hello to Jeff."

Me: "Hello, Jeff, pleasure to meet you. She sure is very sweet to look at, huh? How would you like to have ***that*** walking around your house all day?"

Jeff: "But you said that ***she*** was his wife. So, then, how are ***you*** with him? I'm confused."

Vivian: "We're together, if you know what I mean. It's one of ***those*** things." She winked at him.

Jeff: "Oh, ok, that's cool. Have a great night, folks." He walked away.

Olivia: "That was classic, girl. You did great." We laughed.

Vivian: "Did you like that, honey? I'm ***so*** done dealing with guys. I will ***never*** be someone's piece of ass ever again."

Me: "You did good, Vivian. I'm very proud of you. From now on I don't want ***any man's*** hands on you ever again, unless they're mine. ***I*** will take care of you from now on. You're off limits to everyone."

Vivian: "Oh really. Can you promise me that? Huh, Julian? Because if you can, then we have a deal."

Olivia: "Yes, girl, he can promise you that. I'll vouch for him" She looks at me and winks.

We finally got seated, and within a few minutes, we all ordered our meals. I told Olivia and Vivian to have as many drinks as they wanted. I was going to be driving home, and the ladies deserved to tie one on. I wasn't much of a drinker, but the ladies sure did love their wine. Our food eventually arrived, and we were all hungry, so we dug in. I just loved the homemade bread in the basket and told the waitress to keep it coming.

Me: "You know, I'm going to tell you again, for the record. You two are the most beautiful ladies here, and it's a pleasure to have you both by my side."

Olivia: "Oh, honey, you're so sweet. You're very flattering. Thank you."

Vivian: "Those are words that I've hardly ever heard before. So, coming from you, Julian, they mean the world to me. I can tell just by talking with you that you are old fashioned and have old fashioned standards and morals."

Olivia: "Oh, honey, Julian ***only*** says what he means. We're going to have to work on that complex that you have, because you really do not have any reason to feel that you're unworthy of anything. A lady like you is very hard to come by these days."

Me: "She's right, Vivian. She and I ***both*** see something very special and unique in you. Perhaps you coming to visit us is a sign of better things to come."

Vivian: "You're going to make me cry. Please, not now. Please."

Olivia: "Ok, girl, not now. We don't want to upset you."

Vivian: "Don't get me wrong, I love your words. I just don't want to lose my composure out in public."

Me: "Ok, let's just enjoy our meals and time together. We have plenty of time to get into personal feelings."

After we finished our meals, we went and sat at the bar for one last drink before we left. Olivia was feeling a little frisky, so we had our hands all over each other, nothing too obvious, but she did rub my crotch briefly as she had her hand on my thigh. I didn't want Vivian to feel left out so I put my arms around her too and pulled her close to me. She smelled so nice, and I loved having her body so close to mine. As we all know, people can become brave and daring when they've had enough alcohol in them.

When we got back home, the ladies changed into something more comfortable, as did I. They wanted to keep drinking their wine, and there was no harm in that. They were home, safe and secure.

Olivia: "That was a very nice dinner. Thank you, honey."

Vivian: "Yes, thank you, Julian."

Me: "You're both quite welcome. I'm glad I got some pictures of you both in those mini dresses before you took them off. You were driving me crazy with those on."

Olivia: "Usually when we get back home from going out, he starts ripping my clothes off at the door on our way to the bedroom."

Vivian: "Well, don't let ***me*** ruin your fun. Have at it."

Olivia: "I'm sure you don't want to hear us having sex, girl. We can hold off for now."

Vivian: "I've heard you two have sex just about every night since I've been here. How else am I going to squirt one off?"

Olivia: "I'm sorry you had to hear that. Are we really ***that*** loud?"

Vivian: "No, girl, ***you're*** really that loud. Either he has a huge dick, or you're still as tight as you were when you were a virgin."

Olivia: "Well, I can assure you that my pooter's not tight anymore, so..."

Me: "Umm, can we not talk about my cock. You're making me blush. It's not huge. Obviously, she's not seasoned enough yet."

Vivian: "Are you sure about that? Because the other night, I heard her tell you that she just loves sucking every veiny inch of your big dick."

Olivia: "Ok, now I'm really embarrassed." She chuckled.

Vivian: "Don't be embarrassed, girl. Just be thankful that you have a man who really knows how to fuck you good enough to get you off."

Me: "Ok, we need to stop talking about sex here. Maybe it's the wine talking, right?"

Olivia: "I suppose you're right, honey. I'm sorry about that."

Me: "It's ok, we're all friends here."

We all settled on the pullout sofa trying to find a good movie to watch. I have so many DVDs that it won't be hard to find a decent flick. Olivia and Vivian were so tipsy from all the wine they drank, that chances are they are going to pass out soon anyways.

Olivia: "Honey, do you want me to scratch your back for you? I know how you love that feeling."

Me: "Oh, hell yes. You ***never*** have to ask me."

I was lying on my belly, and Olivia sat on top of me and started scratching my back. I took off my T-shirt and just laid there while she dug her nails into my skin. Vivian was lying next to us having a smoke and sipping her wine. Both of the ladies only had on T-shirts with no bras, and very sexy panties. I kept staring at the tattoos on Vivian's thighs. It was very hard not to notice them.

Vivian: "Do you have any porn videos by any chance."

Olivia: "Umm, ***no***, we don't. Are you getting horny, girl?"

Vivian: "No, not really. Porn videos may be the only sexual satisfaction I get while I'm here. I'm about due to go squirt one off." She chuckled.

Me: "But you said that you've heard us having sex all the time since you've been here. Didn't ***that*** get you off? I thought for sure it would have."

Vivian: "Oh, so you were ***hoping*** that I heard you two going at it. It's kind of hard not to hear loud, deep moaning in the middle of the night. Are you trying to rub in?"

Me: "No, not at all. I'm actually quite surprised that you could hear us from the bedroom in the apartment."

Vivian: "I didn't say that I was in bed when I heard you. Maybe I was laying right here on this sofa."

Olivia: "Or maybe you were right outside our bedroom door. ***You were, weren't you, girl?*** You can tell us. We don't care if you were, as long as it's not morbid for you to hear us having sex."

Vivian: "Now, why would I do ***that***?" She gives a wink.

We changed the subject and were now talking about when Vivian was leaving, which was in the next day or two. Vivian didn't want to leave, but she had to go home and get back to work. She was a waitress during the day, and a bar tender at night. She was getting quite burnt out by it, and desperately wanted a positive change in her life. That's why she valued and adored her relationship with Olivia and me. She really didn't want to be away from us, and we really wanted her to consider coming back soon for good. I got off the sofa and headed to the bathroom.

Olivia: "Viv, can you make it back for Christmas, by any chance?"

Vivian: "I don't know. I can't promise you anything right now. My life is in shambles, and I need to get a grip on it."

Olivia: "Are you happy with your life, Vivian? I mean, ***really*** happy with your life?"

Vivian: "Honestly, no, I'm miserable, girl, and I hate my life. Nothing ever seems to go right for me. It's like I keep chasing my tail."

Olivia: "Honey, go home and take care of business, do what you have to do, but please consider coming back for good. We have something very special between us, and to be separated again at this point in our lives, is just unacceptable as far as I'm concerned."

Vivian: "Does Julian know about our past together? Have you told him about us being lovers in high school?"

Olivia: "I did tell him that you were my very first kiss, and that we did have a history together. He wasn't put off by that at all. He knows what we mean to each other, and he also knows that you would never try to come between him and I. He's very fond of you, honey. He adores you, as do I. One thing I know about my precious Julian is that when he loves something, or someone, it's for a very good reason. He doesn't love just ***anybody***."

Vivian: "Olivia, you have such an amazing man. You need to marry him, girl. If you don't, then I will."

Olivia: "We ***are*** getting married, in a few months, Valentine's Day to be exact. So, I will need you to be my maid of honor. If you can't make it back by Christmas, ***please*** be here for my wedding. It will just be a few of us for the ceremony, in our new house. Can I count on you to be here?"

Vivian: "You ***know*** you can, girl. I'll do ***anything*** for you and Julian."

Olivia: "You know we both love you, right?"

Vivian: "I do know that, and I love you both too. Why am I having such a hard time packing up to leave?"

Olivia: "It must be a sign of things to come, girl."

The next day, I got home from work and hopped in the shower while dinner was in the oven. The ladies both seemed a little off today, and I was curious if there was something wrong, so I asked them. They were sad because Vivian was leaving tomorrow morning, and they hadn't come to grips with it yet. I didn't want Vivian to leave either, she grew on me, and I took a great liking to her. It's the kind of feeling parents get when they send their children off to college. You always want them to be safe, healthy, prosperous, and always have money to buy food. I knew what the ladies were going through because once Vivian leaves, who knows how long it will be before we see her again if we do. All I know is that it was going to crush them if they ever got separated again. I'm sure that when they were in high school, their feelings for each other were not as strong or mature as they were experiencing now.

Vivian: "Well, I'm all packed up and ready to leave in the morning. I have to be honest here, I'm really not looking forward to it. I need a glass of wine to calm my nerves, maybe a few of them. This is a lot harder than I anticipated."

Me: "Vivian, we know that you have things to deal with at home, and you have your own life going on there. I don't personally know how happy of a life you live, but I can promise you that if you do come back to stay, we will create the most beautiful life for you. I saw my perfect life many times in my dreams, and I was able to create it in real life. I've had dreams about you since you've been here, and I can say without any reservation that in my heart of hearts, you belong here with me and Olivia. I think you may know that too."

Olivia: "Oh, honey, your way with words just melts my heart. I love you so much, Julian. I also love the world you have created for me, for us. Your love is so precious to me, baby, you know that."

Vivian: "***That right there, is what I want!*** I want to be told every day that I'm loved and needed. I want the same kind of love that you two have. Why is it ***so*** hard to find it? I've tried everything I know just to feel important to someone. Why have I not found it? ***Why?*** "

Olivia: "Viv, you're not giving yourself enough credit. Just be patient, girl. You ***will*** have it. You will. There is no way that you will not have the same kind of love that Julian and I have."

Vivian: "I know it's early, but I'm going to call it a night after I finish this glass of wine. I have so much on my mind right now, and I need to get some sleep before I get a migraine. I love you both. I just want you to know that."

Me: "We love you too, Vivian. Sleep well."

Olivia: "Good night, honey. We'll see you in the morning."

Morning came, and all three of us were having our after-breakfast smoke and coffee. Vivian will be leaving shortly, and things are a little emotional right now. I had her car all packed and ready to go, but she was taking her time getting ready to leave. This was going to crush Olivia, and they were both already crying. I didn't know what to do, so I just held them both very close to me. Both of their heads were buried in my chest. I kept kissing the top of their heads and rubbing their backs. A woman is so strong when it comes to comforting a man, but when the roles are reversed, I'm sure most men struggle with comforting a woman; I know ***I*** was.

Vivian: "Ok, it's time. I better leave while I still have the power to." She cried again.

Olivia: "I understand, honey. Just please know that we love you and we will think about you all the time. Girl, you're my best friend, and I adore you."

Me: "Please make sure you call us when you get home, and here's an envelope with some cash in it, in case you need it."

Vivian: "Honey, I don't need money, but thank you so much for this. Julian, you're an amazing man, and thank you again for loving my best friend the way you do. She's so fortunate to have you."

We walked out to Vivian's car and gave each other one last hug and kiss. Vivian and Olivia cried again, but it was more like a proud cry. They kissed again, and Vivian finally got in her car and started it up. Olivia and I walked down the driveway towards the house, up onto the deck and stopped at the front door. When we turned and looked down at the driveway, Vivian was still there, staring at us. I saw her piercing blue eyes clearly through the windshield. Finally, she stuck out her hand and waved goodbye.

Chapter 8 – The Crush That Kills

It has been two weeks since Vivian left, and Olivia is still quite sad about saying goodbye to her best friend. She was very strong at keeping her composure, but she did have her moments when she needed a hug and some comfort to keep away the tears. Christmas was in two and a half weeks, and it was going to be our first one together. We hadn't thought much about moving over to the new house for good, so we decided to have our first Christmas in the old place, where we were. We had so many precious memories here and it was becoming hard to make the transition over to the new place. Vivian and Olivia talked every day on the phone, sometimes several times a day. It was very gratifying for them. One night Olivia and I were lying in bed talking about our sexy Vivian.

Olivia: "Honey, I miss her so much. I wish she was still here with us. I worry so much about her, hoping that she's safe and warm."

Me: "I miss her too, babe. Did she mention if she was coming back for Christmas?"

Olivia: "She did say that if she couldn't be here for Christmas, she would definitely be here to celebrate our marriage with us. She's my maid of honor. So, ***that's*** something to look forward to."

Me: "You two have a very special bond, don't you? A genuine love for each other."

Olivia: "We do, honey, yes. And it's not just because she was my first kiss. We were born to be best friends, I think. I have to be honest here; I'm pleasantly surprised that you're so at ease with her and I being past lovers. When I told you that, I was so worried that you would have a hard time trusting her and I together."

Me: "Honey, I know that you and Vivian had a thing for each other in high school, and I'm cool with that. I want you to be happy, and if it means spending time with her, then I'm quite alright with that. I know you'll never take my trust in you for granted, or I would have never put that beautiful ring on your finger."

Olivia: "Would it bother you if I told you that once or twice as we were making love, I thought about her being on top of me instead of you?"

Me: "No, not at all. In fact, if we're being honest here, I did fantasize about sleeping with her as we were making love. Of course, I've wondered how good she is at sucking dick, and how good she moves that ass in bed. There's no way I could look at her and not ponder those thoughts."

Olivia: "I remember one time, when we were making out in her bedroom, she asked me if I would consider strapping on a dildo and doing her with it. She wasn't a virgin, by far. So, that's what I did. Maybe that's too much information, I'm sorry."

Me: "It's ok, honey. She was a part of your life, and now she has come back into it. That can ***only*** be very beautiful, right?"

Olivia: "Yes, very beautiful. Honey, I'm not looking to go to bed with her again, honest. My heart belongs to you, and you ***know*** that. Before you came into my life, she was the only good memory that I had growing up."

All that talk about Vivian was getting us both very horny. So, as we were making love, Vivian's name was mentioned quite a bit. We did it on purpose, to spice things up a little bit. We wanted to see how long it would take us both to get off while talking about the red headed bombshell. As always, Olivia and I always kissed a lot as we made love. She also has a tendency to talk to me as I'm fucking her. This was one of those times.

Olivia: "I miss her so much, baby. I wish she was right here, right now."

Me: "In bed with us?"

Olivia: "Yes, watching us make love. You want that too, don't you?"

Me: "That would be such a turn on. I would love to see her pleasure herself in front of us."

Olivia must have been super horny, because she kept pulling more of my cock inside of her.

Olivia: "She's so beautiful and sexy. I don't want anyone else to have her besides us. Yes?"

Me: "Yes. Just us, babe."

Olivia: "If she comes back, do you promise to help me keep her here?"

Me: "You know that I will, honey."

We got heavily into kissing. Olivia loves it when we kiss, and I suck on her bottom lip. That drives her crazy. She was sucking on my neck and left a couple of red "*love marks*." I did the same thing to her when I was sucking on her neck.

Olivia: "Do you want her as much as I do? Huh? Do you? Tell me. Tell me that you want to fuck her."

Me: "You know that I do, babe. Don't you?"

Olivia: "Oh yes, I can tell that you do."

I could tell that Olivia was close to squirting because the tone of her voice changed, and she wanted me to go faster. For a moment there, I was the one trying to keep up with her.

Me: "If you never met me, would you want to be with Vivian?"

Olivia: "***Ooh, yeah, honey!*** I would want her very badly. Would you want her if you never met me? Huh? Would you want her mouth on your cock instead of mine?"

Me: "Yes, every day."

That was enough to send Olivia over the edge. She pulled me in all the way, and I felt her squirting. Less than thirty seconds later she felt me cum inside her. She had a very firm grip on my ass, making sure that I couldn't pull out, even if I wanted to. She was biting the side of my neck softly, trying to calm down her deep moaning. When we were done making love, as usual, we kissed for some time. We were still talking about Vivian, and how incredibly sexy we both thought she was. She's the hottest looking redhead, ever, in my opinion. Everything about her is sexy. If I wasn't with Olivia, I would definitely want to be with Vivian. But then again, if I had never met Olivia, I would have no idea that Vivian even existed.

Olivia: "I need a smoke now, baby. Care to join me?"

Me: "Sure thing."

Olivia: "Wow, that sure was intense, sweetheart. That was certainly different, huh? That was a good ride, baby. Did you enjoy it as much as I did?"

Me: "I enjoyed it very much, my love. I ***always*** enjoy being inside you."

Olivia: "I love how you just let me be myself, sweetheart. You never judge me, and I love you for that."

Me: "I'm actually quite surprised that when you and Vivian were kissing in her bedroom, that she didn't do ***you*** with a strap-on. Or did she?"

Olivia: "No. I really wanted nothing to do with actual sex, but I really did enjoy all of the kissing and tit feeling. Truth be told, I did her several times with a strap-on, but never, did she ever do me. The farthest she ever got with me was putting a finger or two inside me. That was more than enough to get me off. We almost got caught by her mother one time." She chuckled.

Me: "Vivian told me that she looks ***just*** like her mother, so her mother must be one hot ass looking lady. Am I right?"

Olivia: "Oh, yeah. Gail is very beautiful. They could pass for identical twins, easily. Unfortunately, Vivian's sister looks more like her dad, and I'm not saying that as a bad thing. She's pretty, too."

Me: "I could really see how excited you were to have Vivian here, and vice- versa. Nothing makes me happier than seeing you smile."

Olivia: "Sweetheart, have I told you how much I love and adore you?"

Me: "Umm, yeah, every day, girl."

Olivia: "I want to get pregnant so bad. I know I keep telling you that. As much as we have sex, one of your seeds is ***bound*** to *"slip past the goalie"* and impregnate me."

Me: "Well, if it's any consolation, honey, I'm more than willing to have sex with you several times a day to make that happen." She chuckled.

Olivia: "The problem with that is, you go for so long, and having sex several times a day makes it almost impossible to walk afterwards. I literally walk around this house all day with a very sore pussy. But you love that. ***Don't you, baby?*** "

Me: "I'm proud to say that I do. If you weren't so damn beautiful and sexy, then I might ease up on you a bit. Watching you walk around in your sexy maid's outfit drives me fucking insane."

Olivia: "See that? I just ***knew*** you were fucking the maid." We laughed.

I had to work in the morning, so I wanted to get some sleep. Olivia was a little tired too from having such an explosive orgasm. The sheets were completely soaked from Olivia's cum, but we didn't care, and we didn't change them right away. When I got up the following morning, Olivia was already up and having her coffee and smoke at the table, waiting for me. I didn't hear her get up, so I must have been very tired, because usually, I'm a very light sleeper, and I'm the first one up.

Olivia: "There's my sexy man. Good morning, baby, I love you."

Me: "And I love you, my precious girl." We kissed good morning.

Olivia: "You know, when I woke up this morning and turned over to face you, you had a huge fucking hard on. I almost put it in my mouth and was going to wake you up with a nice blow job, but I knew you needed your sleep. Who were you thinking about in your dreams that got you so hard, baby? Was it me, or was it Vivian?"

Me: "It must have been you, honey. You're ***all*** I ever dream about."

Olivia: "You don't have to dream about me anymore, sweetheart. I am your reality now, and that's a whole lot better. Right?"

Me: "That is correct. It's probably going to be a very long day for me. I have to finish up on my current build so I can move on to the next one. I guess when you're very good at what you do, word of mouth travels fast. I have a few more jobs to quote this upcoming week. By the looks of it, I'll be very busy well into next Summer."

Olivia: "Honey, I love your deep drive and desire to build. I'm so proud of you for having all that energy to create things. I envy you for that."

Me: "We all have our own desires and talents. You, for instance, have a great knack for crafting things. That may be your calling, honey. You're also very talented at interior design."

Olivia: "My calling was to be with you, honey. Everything else is just secondary as far as I'm concerned."

So, while I was at work, Olivia put her infamous maid's outfit on and tidied up the house. She was on the phone with Vivian as she was cleaning the kitchen. Vivian was on the speaker phone and that freed up Olivia's hands.

Vivian: "Girl, I have some news for you if you're interested in hearing it."

Olivia: "Of course, I am. What is it? Are you coming down soon? Please tell me that you are. Julian and I have been thinking of you non-stop since you left."

Vivian: "Does that mean while you're in bed as well? Because if it does, then you need to fill me in on that." She chuckled.

Olivia: "Yes, that too, if you must know." She chuckled.

Vivian: "***Ooh!*** Now you have my undivided attention. Please tell me it was sexual."

Olivia: "Well, if you must know, last night when we made love, we were both fantasizing about you being in bed with us. I can't believe I'm telling you this."

Vivian: "Who was fucking me? You, or him? Was it a ménage a` trois fantasy? ***I have to know now!*** This is all I'm going to be thinking about now." She chuckled.

Olivia: "We ***both*** were, and he was ***so into it!*** We both talked about you long enough to get us both off really good. The sheets were completely soaked in cum. Do you see what you do to us, Viv?"

Vivian: "***Sure!*** The moment I leave you, ***then*** you both decide to take me to bed. Do you think it was easy for me being there and hearing the bed rattle as you two were going at it, every night?" She chuckled.

Olivia: "It was all just hot foreplay and words, you know. We would never expect that to happen in real life. We were just being curious."

Vivian: "You know, not for nothing, but while I was there, either one of you could have had your way with me. I'm not insinuating that I want to fuck your soon to be husband, because I would never do that to you. I think you know that. There was this magnetizing feeling that came over me, trying to pull me closer to becoming intimate with you and Julian. I know that sounds fucked up."

Olivia: "You don't have to explain anything to me. I felt completely different the moment I got here. Something in the back of my mind was telling me that if I wanted Julian, he was mine for the taking."

Vivian: "Not to change our juicy subject, but how would you feel about me coming for Christmas? Is that something you would entertain?"

Olivia: "You better not be teasing me, girl. If you're serious, we would ***love*** to entertain you again. We've missed you so much, Vivian. It was like a part of our lives were missing the moment you left."

Vivian: "I'm very serious about this. I'm coming to see you two again, and I've been doing nothing but counting the minutes. When I left there, I cried all the way home, and at one point, I stopped my car and turned around. I should have never left there; I felt so alive."

Olivia: "Julian and I were talking about you, and we don't want you to be anywhere else but with us. I know that sounds selfish, but I don't think any of us could deny that there's definitely a very serious connection between us. And if I'm being honest here, the connection is on an intimate level."

Vivian: "Well, if it's ok with Julian, I could be there within three days. But please make sure it's ok with him first. I do not want to overstep my bounds."

Olivia: "Let's have a three-way call with him right now. Ok? Do you know how to do it? I have no idea how to do it, so you'll have to guide me through it."

So, while I was at work, Olivia called me, but she didn't tell me that Vivian was also on the phone. She wanted to get my honest opinion on having Vivian come back. She was also hoping that I would say *"yes,"* because if Vivian heard me say *"no,"* then that would definitely hurt her feelings.

Olivia: "Hi, baby, do you have a few minutes to talk to me?"

Me: "Honey, I have more than a few minutes for you; the rest of my life, actually. What's up, my love?"

Olivia: "I was talking to Vivian earlier, and she wanted to know if she could spend Christmas with us. If so, she could be here within three days. Are you ok with that, honey, and please be honest."

Me: "Well, I don't know if having her here in a few days is a good idea."

Olivia: "Why, baby? Did she say or do something to offend you while she was here? I'm confused."

Me: "Well, honey, it's like this. You just said she could be here in a few days, right?"

Olivia: "I did, yes."

Me: "Well, why do we have to wait a few days to see her? Why can't she come later tonight? Or tomorrow morning. I will pay to fly her out here. Can she do that?"

Olivia: "Well, why don't you ask her, she's on the other line."

Vivian: "Hi, Julian."

Me: "Umm, ***what***? ***Vivian***?"

Vivian: "It's me, honey. Olivia didn't want to tell you that I was on the line too. You really had me biting my nails there for a minute. So, can I come home to you and Olivia? Please, honey? I need to be there with you two."

Me: "Yes, of course you can, girl. But we don't want to wait three more days to see you. You have no idea how much we've missed you and talked about you. Olivia and I had a heart-to-heart talk about you earlier."

Vivian: "You did, huh? Are you referring to when you and Olivia were making love while talking about me? Huh? Is ***that*** the conversation you're referring to? Apparently, from what I heard, you both had very explosive orgasms; another thing I got left out on." She chuckled.

Olivia: "I ***had*** to tell her, baby. It was such an explosive endeavor."

Me: "Yes, that's the one. So, now you know. So, get your sweet ass here as soon as you can."

Olivia: "Thank you, baby, so much."

Vivian: "I think you're starting to feel very deeply for me, Julian. ***Aren't you?*** "

Me: "No, not really. I mean, you're "ok" looking, but that's where I my fondness for you stops."

Vivian: "Julian, you are ***so full of shit!*** Admit it, you love me. You love me like Olivia does."

Olivia: "Of course he does, girl. Don't you, baby?"

Me: "Did you say something, honey? I think the phone's breaking up." They laughed.

Vivian: "Ok, we'll see about that, ***smart ass!*** I'm going to look so smoking hot and sexy for Olivia, that you'll be begging for my attention. And this time, I'm bringing my toys because if you two can cum all over your bed sheets, then I'm going to squirt my ass off too."

Me: "Oh, Vivian, you are a rare bird. We would love to have you. I've got to get back to work. Get here when you can and drive safely. Call us when you're on your way. We love you."

Vivian: "I love you too, honey. Bye."

Olivia: "Bye, baby, I love you. See you soon."

Me: "Goodbye, my love."

Fast forwarding a few days, Vivian was due to arrive any minute now, and Olivia was waiting patiently for her on the deck having a glass of wine and a smoke. Vivian sent her a text stating that she was about five minutes away. Olivia yelled in the house to me saying that Vivian was just about here, so I came outside and sat with Olivia on the two-person swing. A few minutes later, in pulls Vivian, and Olivia's eyes just lit up. We walked down the driveway and met her by the car. She got out and we all hugged and kissed like we hadn't seen each other in years. The kisses were very intense and long.

We helped her unload her car, and then we all had a drink to celebrate her return. She only brought two bags of luggage with her, so she must not plan on staying with us. We were all sitting at the table having a smoke and a drink. She looked absolutely stunning. I've missed looking at her to be honest. I know Olivia was ecstatic to see her again as well. Olivia was feeling quite lonely without her best friend being here. But that was no longer an issue.

Olivia: "How have you been, girlfriend? Anything new and exciting?"

Vivian: "I've been great, and there's nothing new to report. I did miss the shit out of you two though. It was very tough being home after leaving here."

Me: "Well, it's nice to see you again. It will be a wonderful Christmas this year. It's mine and Olivia's first one together, and you being here makes it even more special."

Vivian: "I've missed you so much, you have no idea. I dreaded driving home when I left here. It felt as though I had just left my world behind."

Vivian went into the apartment to unpack, and Olivia didn't feel like cooking, so I decided to take the ladies out for dinner. It took the ladies about thirty minutes to get ready as I was in the shower. I was dressed in five minutes flat. They were both in the apartment finishing up, and then they both came strutting out in sexy hip hugger jeans and very nice sweaters. They looked incredibly sexy and were both wearing the *"Angel"* perfume. Vivian, like Olivia, didn't wear too much make-up. These ladies had classic beauty. They rolled out of bed looking beautiful. We had a quick smoke, and then headed out. We took Olivia's Blazer, and I drove. When we got to the restaurant and were walking towards the entrance, we were all holding hands. We didn't want Vivian to feel left out. We got plenty of looks from people who were leaving the place as we walked in. We were seated and had a drink before ordering our food. I sat across from both of them.

Vivian: "Julian, thanks for taking us out for dinner, this is a very nice place."

Olivia: "We came here before and loved the food. I think it was our first night out, wasn't it honey?"

Me: "It was. You ladies order whatever you want, don't be shy. It's my treat."

Vivian: "Do you two have all of your Christmas shopping done?"

Olivia: "I have most of it done. There are a few things I'm still waiting for. This is the best time of the year, at least I think so. It's definitely the most beautiful, and this will be the best ever Christmas for me because it's the first one with my honey. I love you so much, baby."

Me: "And I love you. And we both love you, Vivian, you know that, right?"

Vivian: "I do, and I love you both very much. I thought about you all the time. It was hard to focus on anything else, but I got through it."

The tables were kind of close together, so we didn't know how much of what we were saying was being heard by other people there. And to be honest, we didn't really care either. We'll give them something to talk about. I'm quite sure that most of the men in here having dinner with their wives or girlfriends are checking the ladies out. I have yet to bring Olivia to a place where she did not get eye fucked by someone. I'm sure Vivian gets the same attention wherever she goes too.

Olivia: "Viv, tomorrow I have a lot of running around to do, if you want to come with me."

Vivian: "Sure, it will be fun. I have a couple of places I would like to stop at too if that's ok."

Olivia: "Absolutely. We'll go while Julian's at work. Honey, do you need anything while we're out? I know that we're out of the razor blades that we use to shave our privates."

Vivian: "***Mm!*** That's an interesting visual." She gives me a wink.

Me: "I can't think of anything. But between now and then I'm sure I'll remember something. Or I'll remember after you have already returned home."

Vivian: "My peach is starting to itch. That must mean it's time for a shave again. It's not like it has seen any action lately."

Olivia: "Oh, I know the feeling girl. But my sweet Julian loves a shaved pooter, so I deal with the itching."

Vivian: "Yeah, but at least you have someone to enjoy your shaved pooter. I don't think my dildos care if I'm shaved or not." She chuckled.

I ordered a bottle of wine for our table. I knew how much the ladies loved their wine; way more than I did, that's for sure. I ordered a White Russian. Vivian was telling us what she had been up to since she left. She hadn't mentioned staying with us yet.

Me: "Vivian, have you given any thought to staying in the house when we move to the new one?"

Vivian: "Um, yes, but I'm very hesitant because it would bother me if I felt like any kind of a burden to you two. I'm being honest with you."

Olivia: "Oh honey, you wouldn't be a burden at all, we told you that. We want you to live there."

Our food arrived at the table, and we dug in. The ladies both had Chicken French, while I had the Chicken Armando, which was a new item on the menu.

Me: "***Damn!*** You ladies smell incredible, I just love that perfume. We'll be stocking up on it." Olivia winked at me.

Olivia: "Well, I know what I'm getting for Christmas. Huh, baby?"

Me: "No, that would ruin the surprise now, wouldn't it? Vivian, is there anything in particular you'd like for Christmas?"

Vivian: "Um, something that's not too big to fit in my purse, or in my ass." She winks.

Olivia: "Something big enough to gnaw on?"

Vivian: "Can you find me one for Christmas? Something with some real girth to it that's going to make me cross my eyes when it's inside me?"

Olivia: "I know where there's one." They chuckled.

We needed to finish our meals before someone called the manager on us and we were asked to leave the restaurant. That would be embarrassing, even though I knew the manager and our waitress.

Vivian: "You know, I don't usually talk this way unless I'm hanging around you two. You must be a bad influence on me. Aren't you both ashamed of yourselves?"

Olivia: "Do we have to be? Because we're not."

Me: "No, not at all. That's how we talk to each other. And besides, foreplay lasts all day."

Vivian: "***Ooh!*** Is this a sign of big things to come in the near future?"

We finished our meals and headed home. We did stop off and grab some more wine for the ladies; a case of it to be exact. I actually bought a case of it two weeks ago but wrapped it up and put it under the tree for Olivia. But since Vivian was here, I just changed the tag and put both of their names on it. When we got home, we all changed into something more casual to lounge around in.

Olivia: "I want to find a good horror movie to watch and chill on the pull-out sofa. Sound good?"

Vivian: "Oh yeah, that's fine. I'm a little exhausted from the drive, so this sofa feels very good."

We did find a good movie to watch, but since the ladies were quite tipsy from all of the wine, it didn't take long for them to pass out. I wasn't overly tired, but I tried my best to get some sleep, so that's where we all fell asleep. When morning came, I was the first one up, so I hopped in the shower while the coffee was brewing. I'm sure the ladies were going to sleep in for quite a while yet because they did drink a lot of wine last night.

I went out to the garage once I got a cup of coffee and had a smoke. I was working on a motor that I had got from the scrap yard. All of the machine work was done to it, and it was ready to be rebuilt. It was originally a spare motor for the Z/28, but I had been wanting to get an older Chevy truck to build. I absolutely love the older chevy square body trucks and have been wanting one for quite some time now. I just haven't found the one that reached out to me and told me to buy it yet. I know it's weird to think this way, but I firmly believe that if you're looking for something in particular to buy, as soon as you see it, something telepathically happens, and you just know that it's the one for you. I've experienced that feeling many times through the years when I was looking to buy a guitar or amp. At that point, it becomes sentimental to you.

I mentioned the word sentimental because it was the same feeling I got when I met Olivia and Vivian. Something deep inside me told me that Olivia and I were purposely made for each other. I had that feeling the moment I met her at the hotel. I got the same feeling when I met Vivian. And because Olivia has a history with her, that fondness rubbed off on me immediately. For whatever reason she was here, I knew that she was not someone that I would ever want to let get away from us. Whatever it was that brought Vivian here only told me that she wanted the same introverted and reclusive life that me and Olivia shared. She was meant to be in our lives.

After being in the garage for about two hours, I went inside the house to fill my coffee cup and both Olivia and Vivian were sitting at the table having coffee and a smoke. They both looked extremely hung over; sexy, but definitely hung over.

Me: “Well, good morning, ladies. How are you today?”

Olivia: “Honey, it feels like a train is driving through my head right now. Did we really drink that much wine last night? ***Shit!*** “

Me: “You had quite a bit, baby. And how do you feel, Vivian?”

She just looked at me with those beautiful, piercing eyes and stared at me. She finally responded, although it seemed like quite the effort to do so.

Vivian: “I kind of feel like I’m still drunk, to be honest. But there is great comfort in knowing that Olivia is sharing the same headache with me.”

Olivia: “I remember getting home from the restaurant, and that’s about it. Honey, come give me a kiss and please bring me some aspirin.”

Me: “Sure, babe. Is there anything else you need?”

Vivian: “I’ll take a kiss and some aspirin too, if you don’t mind.”

Me: “You ladies were close to being drunk when you left the restaurant. You had a good time though, and that’s what matters, right? Hey, how about if I fire up the hot tub? Would that wake you up and make you feel better?”

Olivia: “Umm, I think a cold shower will do the trick. Vivian, you’re more than welcome to sit in the hot tub if you like.”

Vivian: “No, honey. I’d probably fall asleep in it and drown.” She chuckled.

Me: “I’m going to make you both a nice breakfast. I’ll put another pot of coffee on too. Just relax and let me take care of you.”

Olivia: "Oh baby, I just adore you. You take such great care of me."

Vivian: "He sure does love his lady. Can I get pampered too?" She chuckled.

Olivia: "Do you need some love and affection too, Vivian?"

Vivian: "I do, yes. And he did promise me that he would take care of me as long as I never allowed another man to put his hands on me. And right now, I need a lot of attention."

Me: "I'll tell you what; I have a friend who does deep tissue massages. I'm going to call her and see when I can get you both in. Does that sound like something you would be interested in?"

Olivia: "That would feel ***awesome***, honey. I've never had one before."

Vivian: "Girl, you're going to love it, I promise you that."

Me: "So, should I call her?"

Olivia: "I'm in, how about you, Viv?"

Vivian: "Absolutely. I hope she's hot looking." They laughed.

Me: "Oh, she's quite the looker, but I know for a fact that she's not bi-sexual. So, you'll have to pass on her, Vivian."

Vivian: "I'm not looking to hook up with her, Julian. Don't even think about that for a minute. I was just being a smart ass."

Me: "I'm well aware of you being a smart ass, girl."

Vivian: "Keep it up, Julian. And remember, you said I was just "*ok*" looking, so you are not allowed to touch me while I'm here. And I ***know*** that you've been staring at my peach."

Olivia: "You two bicker as if ***you're*** the ones getting married." We laughed.

Once they both took a shower, they felt a lot better. It was obviously going to be a lazy day for all of us, and we really needed it. I just laid on the pullout sofa and was watching music DVDs. It didn't take long for them to snuggle up next to me. Olivia and I were kissing quite a bit as we were talking, and we didn't want Vivian to feel slighted, so we cooled it on that.

Vivian: "It feels ***so good*** to be back here. I feel so safe and secure when I'm with you in this house. I want nothing to do with the outside world, ever again."

Olivia: "Viv, we just want you to know that it was very hard for us when you left. We really missed you."

Vivian: "So, is it safe to assume that you both thought of me as much as I thought of you? I ***could not*** get you off my mind no matter how hard I tried. It was affecting my work habits."

Olivia: "Yes, that's an accurate assumption. I mean, we both fucked our brains out just thinking about you. Let's not forget that."

Vivian: "Truth be told here; I did rub one off thinking about you two as well. Come to think of it, I rubbed off several lately." She chuckled.

I did manage to get ahold of my friend Chelsea, the lady who does massages, and she had several openings this afternoon, so I made the ladies appointments.

Me: "Umm, you ladies better get dressed soon because my friend Chelsea has openings early this afternoon."

Olivia: "Aww, thank you, baby. Thank you so much."

Vivian: "Yes, thank you so much, Julian."

While the ladies were off getting their massages, I started putting more presents under the Christmas tree. I didn't decorate the house too much since we'd be packing up soon to move over to the new house. The ladies did add their elegant touches around here, but it was nothing too crazy. I had everything in my music room pretty much all boxed up and ready to move. I would be selling the house fully furnished if Vivian decided not to stay here when Olivia and I moved over to the new house. Either way, Olivia and I are going to do whatever it takes to keep Vivian here, and active in our lives.

Chapter 9 – Christmas Cuties

It was Christmas morning, and I finally woke up. I heard Christmas music playing out in the living room, so when I walked out of my bedroom, I noticed that Olivia and Vivian both had on sexy, matching Santa's outfits, obviously ones that you would get at an adult lingerie store. They were just having a blast, dancing to the Christmas music, and shaking their ultra-fine asses. We kissed good morning, and I sat at the table drinking my coffee, watching them act like young schoolgirls.

Olivia: "Merry Christmas, baby, I love you so much."

Vivian: "Merry Christmas, Julian. Thanks for having me. This is going to be the best Christmas, ever."

Me: "You both look absolutely stunning, ***and inviting***, I might add."

Vivian: "Oh, really? Look all you want, because you can't touch this, honey." She winked.

Olivia: "You should probably stop teasing him, girl."

Vivian: "How do we look? Is this going to do it for you?"

Me: "Olivia looks incredibly edible, and you look "ok" I suppose."

Vivian: "***Are you kidding me right now? Just "ok"?*** "

Me: "Yeah, you look alright, I guess. You're kind of cute."

Vivian: "***You*** are going to get an ass beating, honey. ***You want this, and you know it!*** "

Olivia: "You know he's only messing with you, girl. Of course, he wants you." She chuckled.

Vivian: "I want to hear him say it. Say it, Julian. Admit that you want me. ***Olivia did!*** "

Me: "Well, I'm sure she does. But ***I'm*** just not feeling it for you. Olivia obviously has different tastes in women than I do, not that she is bi-sexual or anything."

Vivian: "Honey, I'm taking back all the gifts I got you. Tell me. ***Tell me, Julian!*** "

Me: "Ok, Vivian. I love you and I want you. Are you happy now?"

Vivian: "Was that so hard? You know, for someone who told me that he would take care of me, you're not being very considerate of my feelings." We laughed.

Olivia: "Honey, are we going to open the presents after we finish breakfast, or later today? Do you have a preference?"

Me: "Which do you prefer? I'll let you decide."

Olivia: "Let's do them after breakfast, like they're traditionally done."

Me: "And you, Sexy Red? Do you have a preference?"

Vivian: "I'm with Olivia; after breakfast."

Me: "Ok, it's settled. But the ones with the ice cream in them should probably be opened very soon."

Vivian: "***Why in the hell would you gift wrap ice cream?*** "

Me: "There's two of them under there. One for each one of you. So, you better find them quickly ladies, or we will have one hell of a mess to pick up."

Olivia: "***Baby, are you fucking with us?*** You better be fucking with us right now." I chuckled.

Me: "Honestly, I don't remember."

Vivian: "Julian, you're going to get a beat down if you're lying."

Me: "I think I'm kidding, but I'm not sure now."

We finished our breakfast, had a cup of coffee and a smoke, and then started opening gifts. I handed Olivia a present and she opened it up. It was a white gold diamond necklace that read: *"Julian and Olivia, Beyond Forever."* She got a little emotional as she took it out of the box. Vivian placed it on her neck. It looked very nice on her. The lights on the Christmas tree were making it sparkle.

Olivia: "Oh honey, baby, this is so beautiful. Thank you so much."

I handed Vivian a present from both Olivia and I, and it was a white gold bracelet that read: *"The Most Beautiful Love Is Waiting Here for You."*

Vivian: "Oh honeys, thank you so much, I love it, it is stunning. You really didn't have to do this."

Olivia: "You're welcome, girl, we love you. Oh, by the way, Julian, there's a present for you in your music room. Let's do that one next."

I walked towards my music room; they were following me. When I opened the door, there, on a guitar stand was a Gibson Les Paul Black Beauty guitar. I had to step back for a minute, as I looked at them. Those guitars are not cheap, and it's hard enough to find a vintage one.

Me: "***Whoa! Baby, what have you done here?*** There is no way that I'm seeing this right now."

I had to collect my thoughts, and as I was doing that, they were both hugging me. If I wasn't seeing it with my own eyes, I would have never believed it. I tried to speak but I got a little choked up.

Olivia: "Merry Christmas, baby, I love you with all my heart. I heard you mention to one of your friends on the phone that you were looking for this guitar. I'm so glad I found one before you did. Apparently, these vintage guitars are getting very hard to find."

I was almost in tears as I looked at it. I picked it up, strummed on it, and felt the beauty of its neck, the fretless wonder. On the back cavity plate, Olivia signed it with a gold permanent marker, and it read: "*I Am Yours, Beyond Forever*."

Me: "Honey, this is a very expensive guitar, I wish you hadn't spent that much money on me. I'm at a loss for words right now. It's gorgeous and I love it. I don't know what to say, baby."

Olivia: "You deserve this for all you have done for me. If the price was a million dollars, and I had the money, I still would have bought it for you. I love you that much. Do you like the guitar strap on it?"

Me: "I love it. It's beautiful, just like the both of you. I don't deserve this."

The guitar strap had my name embroidered on it, and it was a thick, wide leather strap. I needed a wide one for that guitar because it was very heavy on my shoulder when I played it. The guitar weighed ten pounds, and that might not seem like much until you've played it for a few hours standing up.

Olivia: "Vivian had that made for you, baby."

Me: "You did this for me, Vivian?"

Vivian: "I did, for you, honey. But you weren't getting it until you finally admitted to me that you loved and wanted me." She chuckled.

Me: "I feel like the luckiest man in the world right now. Thank you both, so very deeply."

Olivia: "I love you baby, and I wanted you to have a very special Christmas. You've done so very much for me, and I don't know how I could ever thank you."

Me: "Baby, you've already thanked me by accepting that engagement ring."

Vivian: "That really is a gorgeous ring, girl. ***I wish I was wearing it!*** "

Olivia: "Girl, one day you will be wearing your very own engagement ring from a man that adores you and the ground you walk on. Around here, we turn our dreams into reality. Don't we, baby?"

Me: "We sure do. And Vivian, a man who is worthy of your love and affection, and appreciates the fine lady that you are, is going to steal that precious heart of yours one day, just like you will steal his."

Vivian: "I'm not quite sure that my heart is available anymore for ***any man*** to steal. And besides, you won't ***let*** any man get close enough to me to steal it." We laughed.

Olivia: "She's catching on, honey. Slowly, but surely."

We opened the rest of the presents, and they were mostly clothes and novelty items, a lot of them. I did buy the ladies some very sexy lingerie outfits. I never really know what to buy women for Christmas, so I figured that I couldn't go wrong with jewelry, perfume and gift cards. I'm not much for going out and walking through the malls looking for things to buy. If I can buy things online and have them delivered right to me, I always go that route. Olivia and Vivian, on the other hand, don't mind spending hours shopping and driving around, as long as they're together, and having a good time doing it.

I wanted to capture these precious moments on film, so I had the camcorder sitting on a pedestal the whole time. Since the ladies knew they were being recorded, they just had to do and say provocative things, including dirty dancing and grinding up against each other. It seemed to me at times that they wanted to get a little more physical with each other but pulled away at the last second.

Me: "For a moment there, I thought you two were going to start making out. Don't be teasing me like that because I may just love watching that."

Vivian: "He wants to see us make out, girl."

Olivia: "Yeah, I'm picking up on that too. Honey, is that what you want, to see us get hot and heavy? Do you want to make a video of me and Vivian swapping tongues and feeling each other up?"

Me: "No. I was just saying that because it looked like you were thinking about it for a second. I wouldn't have been overly shocked to see that."

Olivia: "Of course we thought about it, honey. I mean, we do have vested feelings for each other. We just wanted to spice things up a bit for you since you were recording everything."

Vivian: "I probably would have followed through with it, to be honest. The last thing I want is for things to get weird between us, so I backed off."

Olivia: "Girl, you are so fucking hot and sexy. How could ***anyone*** ever resist you?"

Vivian: "I think you have that backwards, Olivia. ***You're*** the hot and heavy around here."

Me: "You're ***both*** elevens on a scale from one to ten." They both puckered their lips at me.

Olivia: "Honey, do you realize that in just two months, we are getting married? That will be the best Valentine's Day ever for me. I'm going to be a basket case, so maybe I should start drinking right now to calm my nerves." She chuckled.

Vivian: "Girl, you'll be just fine. I'm the one who's going to be a basket case, seeing my best friend get married to such an amazing man."

Me: "Well, we're going to keep it very simple. We'll get married in the new house, you'll be Olivia's maid of honor, and my friend Eric will be my best man. We may invite a few close friends, but that's about it. A wedding doesn't have to cost thousands of dollars for it to have real meaning."

Vivian: "Do you know what that means, Olivia?"

Olivia: "No. What does it mean?"

Vivian: "It means that we get to go shopping for our dresses, and you ***know*** how much fun we have when we go shopping together."

Me: "If you ask me, I think you two enjoy shopping just so you can walk around strutting those fine rear ends of yours and teasing all the men."

Vivian: "Who? ***Us!*** We would never do that, would we, girl?"

Olivia: "I don't, but you certainly do, Viv." They laughed.

Me: "Yeah, that sounds like Vivian, to the letter. I haven't known her for too long, but I think I know what she's all about."

Vivian: "It's not ***my fault*** that most men have perverted thoughts when they look at women. Olivia, do you remember when we were at the grocery store and those two guys were following us around? At least, it appeared that that they were. Do you remember that?"

Olivia: "Are you referring to the time when you grabbed my ass and squeezed it when they were walking right behind us?"

Vivian: "Yes. Do you remember the one guy asking the other if he was recording it on his cell phone? Did you hear him say that?"

Olivia: "I do remember that, yes. Is that when you slipped your hand down the back of my pants and held it there, squeezing my ass cheeks?"

Vivian: "Yes, that's it. And when I turned around to look at them, they acted like they were looking for something on the top shelf and walked around us."

Me: "Well, there you have it, ladies. You are **both** top shelf material."

Olivia: "He has such a way with words, doesn't he, Viv?"

Vivian: "***Oh look, it's snowing!*** How beautiful is that? On Christmas morning of all days. ***Aww!*** I have to record this, it's so pretty."

Olivia:" It's a blessing to get snow on Christmas morning."

Me: "Yes, you better record it, because around here we don't get very much snow. It gets a little cold outside, but hardly ever enough snow to mention."

Olivia: "Honey, let's make some hot chocolate and go sit on the deck and watch the snow fall."

Me: "Ok, we can do that. I'm ***assuming*** that we have hot chocolate."

Vivian: "We sure do, quite a bit of it actually."

So, we made our hot chocolates and sat out on the deck, watching the snow fall. We were all sitting on the two-person swing. It's not designed for three people, so it was a little cramped, but we made it work. I was sitting between them, feeling like a sardine in a can, but it was all good. We brought out a blanket and were cuddled up inside of it.

Olivia: "Oh, honey, look at the deer out there. I hope they're not cold and starving."

Me: "That reminds me, babe, I bought some apples for them to eat. Let me up for a second and I'll cut some up for them. Maybe they'll come in real close to the house."

I cut up a whole bag of apples for the deer and started throwing them in the yard, trying to get the deer to notice them. Within a minute, they all walked up closer to us, just on the edge of the yard, which was about fifty feet away. They remembered Olivia hand feeding them, so she and Vivian got very close to them. The baby deer was there again, looking for Olivia. Vivian was able to hand feed the deer too. I stayed back a bit and kept throwing the apples towards them.

Vivian: "Holy shit, that's a huge deer. It won't attack me, will it?"

Olivia: "No, honey, just reach out your hand and let him come to you. He will if he wants that apple bad enough. I'm trying to get close to the baby, but it's so skittish right now. Oh, Viv, look at them. They're so beautiful. I want one." She chuckled.

Vivian: "I want one too."

Olivia: "***Aww! Look at the babies!*** "

Vivian: "They're called fawns, honey. Aren't they adorable?"

Me: "Well, if we keep leaving apples out for them every day, they'll definitely come back. So, if you want to call the deer your own, we need to keep feeding them every day."

Olivia: "It's hunting season too, so they must be very scared and timid right about now. Don't worry, beautiful deer, we'll keep you out of harm's way. They're very safe on this property."

Vivian: "I'm sure they feel quite safe being right in your back yard, where no one can shoot them. If I ever see someone in these woods sneaking up on the deer, I'm going to pump some lead in their ass. So, honey, you'll have to give me a few lessons on firing a shotgun. Can you do that for me?"

Me: "I can do that for you. Olivia should learn to shoot too, as long as we're talking about it. I don't want ***anyone*** messing with my deer, or my ladies."

Olivia: "I just ***love*** how protective you are of us, sweetheart. My man loves, and my man protects."

Vivian: "Well, I hope your man loves me enough to protect me too."

Olivia: "I think you already know that he does, Viv."

Me: "That is correct, as long as she behaves. I'll have to keep a good eye on her."

Vivian: "***Ooh!*** Will you spank me when I'm naughty? Because I do have a history of getting out of hand at times." She chuckled.

Me: "Go ahead, Vivian, get out of hand. You'll be spending the whole day locked in your room."

Vivian: "Would that also include you being on top of me?" She smiles.

Olivia: "Ok, honey, get your mind out of the gutter. We're not done feeding the deer yet. Hey Viv, when we go shopping again, make sure you put apples on our list. Now I feel like I ***have*** to feed them."

Vivian: "You know, the animals around here have it pretty good. They must know that Julian will feed them every day."

Olivia: "Oh yes, he's always feeding the squirrels, bunnies and birds. He just loves animals, and so do I. And if you know what's good for you Vivian, you'll start to love animals too, or you'll have a sore ass."

Vivian: "***Ouch!*** Would that sore ass be from his hand, or his cock? I'm just asking so I know how bad I'm supposed to be." We all laughed.

Olivia: "Girl, you just ***love*** to get laid, don't you?"

Vivian: "Well, ***don't you? Wait!*** I can answer that, since all I've heard since I've been here is you moaning in the middle of the night when I'm trying to sleep." She chuckled.

We finished feeding the deer and they wandered back into the woods. We can't wait to see if they come back tomorrow for some more apples. We had finished our hot chocolates and decided to go back inside for a little while. The sun was starting to show its face so I'm sure we'd be back out on the deck soon enough.

Olivia: "Honey, for dinner we're having stuffed shells. Are you ok with that, or do you want something else?"

Me: "I love stuffed shells, that'll work just fine. I see that you made your homemade bread too. ***Yummy!*** Is there anything that we need from the store?"

Vivian: "I think we're all set. We have enough wine to last us until next year, since you bought us a case for Christmas. You must think we're raging alcoholics." She chuckled.

Olivia: "Well, we do go through a lot of it, girl. We should learn how to make our own. Wouldn't that be fun? We could drink on the job." They laughed.

Me: "I'm sure you ladies would drink it as fast as you made it. We would never have any saved up."

Vivian and Olivia changed out of their sexy Santa outfits and put a couple of my sweatshirts on, along with super tight leggings. As always, they wore that sexy *"Angel"* perfume that I loved to smell. They did a great job on their fingers and toenails. They were red and green with tiny snowflakes on them. Olivia got me more Drakkar cologne because she knew that was all I ever wore.

Olivia: "***Damn, honey!*** You smell so good. I may have to take you to bed really quick. Do you want a quickie, Lover?"

Vivian: "Umm, ***no, you will not!*** If I can't get laid right now, the least you could do is wait until later when I'm in bed sleeping."

Olivia: "Well, what fun would ***that be***? We thought you loved hearing us have sex."

Vivian: "I do, but not during the day when I ***know*** you're heading to your room to get laid. It's a lot more erotic and sexier when I'm caught off guard."

Me: "She's right, babe. It is a little unfair of us to put her through that on a daily basis. But then again, I never see her hopping into bed with us."

Vivian: "***Really!*** And how would you feel about that if I actually did it?"

Olivia: "Girl, as much as we love you, we need to leave sex with you out of the equation."

Vivian: "I know. That's why I brought my trusty toys with me." She chuckled.

Olivia: "Speaking of that, show Julian the sizes of some of your toys. Honey, you won't believe what she stuffs inside that beautiful peach of hers." We laughed.

Me: "You know, I ***did*** notice one of my baseball bats missing from the garage. Do you have it, by any chance, Vivian?"

Vivian: "You're funny, ***honey!*** My peach isn't ***that*** gaping. And besides, I'm sure your baseball bat is made out of wood, and I'd be afraid to get slivers. Do you have any aluminum bats?" We laughed.

Olivia: "Oh, our sweet Vivian. I wouldn't want her any other way."

Me: "Yeah, she is definitely adorable, ***and*** one of a kind."

We made ourselves a drink and went back out on the deck. They love their wine, while I prefer drinking White Russians and Bloody Mary's. The deer were back by the tree line again and I noticed that I was running very low on apples, so I told the ladies to feed them what was left of the apples, and I'd drive into town and grab some more. So, that's what they did as I was gone. I have a friend who owns an apple orchard, and he lets me fill up the back of my truck with them. I pay him a few dollars and I get to take as many as I want, which I'm very grateful for.

Olivia: "Oh, Viv, they're so pretty, aren't they. Look at them, running scared because certain people feel the need to hunt them."

Vivian: "There has to be a good reason why people are allowed to hunt them, otherwise that would be a very cruel thing to do to them. It breaks my heart every time I see one lying on the side of the road dead. I'd much rather see a crooked politician on the side of the road."

Olivia: "Julian gets very upset when he hears guys talk about going out and killing themselves some deer. He has a fondness for animals that I just love."

The deer came back out from the tree line as soon as they saw the ladies throwing apples their way. Olivia and Vivian had acquired a new passion, feeding our deer. They got off the deck and started walking towards the deer very slowly, trying to get closer to their new friends.

Vivian: "Now that they know where they can get something to eat, you may as well consider them your pets because I'm sure they'll be back every day now for the apples. I hope Julian's loading up his truck really good, because we're going to need them."

When I got back home, I saw the ladies out in the yard hand feeding the deer and that melted my heart. I recorded it on my cell phone as I was walking towards the house very quietly. Their bellies must have been full because right as I was walking up the steps of the deck, they trotted away. There were seven of them, including two fawns. I don't know if you've ever heard a baby deer make sounds before, but it is the cutest thing. It reminds me of a toddler learning how to speak.

Olivia: "Honey, did you see me and Vivian hand feeding the deer?"

Me: "I did, yes. That was a very touching moment."

Vivian: "Please tell me that you recorded that."

Me: "I did record it. I will send the video to both of your cell phones, and I'll also download it onto my laptop."

Olivia: "Oh, honey ***that*** was amazing. I was very scared at first. I was shaking."

Vivian: "Me too, girl. But that was a beautiful moment. ***Aww!*** Should we give them names now?"

Olivia: "The fawns were making the cutest sounds. I will never forget this moment, ever."

Me: "The back of my truck is filled with apples, ladies. We've got to find some place to store them all."

Olivia: "We should set aside enough to make a couple of apple pies though. Yes?"

Vivian: "Yes, we should."

Olivia: "Baby, I want them to come back and stay in our yard where I'll know they'll be safe."

Vivian: "They'll come around tomorrow, girl, you'll see."

The sun was out now and the snow that fell would probably be melting away soon. I looked at all the deer tracks coming to and from the house, and that told me that we'd made new friends. Now I feel obligated to keep feeding them every day, just like I do with the birds, squirrels, and bunnies. Last year I had an opossum that came around from time to time. I feel bad for any animal that has to live in the elements and run from the bigger predators to survive. The opossum really loved eating sliced turkey roll, so I stocked up on it for the Winter. It stopped coming around after a while and I can only hope that it's still living and enjoying its life.

Me: "Hey ladies, are you up for taking a walk down the country roads to get some exercise and fresh air? It's not too cold out, or you can stay here if you'd like."

Olivia: "You know I'll go, baby."

Vivian: "That sounds like a great idea."

Me: "Dress warm, ladies. It's a bit chilly out."

We grabbed our smokes, and then we were off. I had a small bottle of Southern Comfort with me to take off the chill in case we needed it. I was drinking it regardless, and I didn't know how fond the ladies were of whiskey. We were all bundled up for the walk. We all had on blue jeans, sweatshirts, Carhartt jackets and hiking boots, which the ladies had just got this morning for Christmas.

Vivian: "Ok, who's holding my hand for this journey?"

Me: "I'll walk in the middle so I can hold hands with both of you. It'll make me feel like a stallion between two mares."

Vivian: "So, you ***are*** hung like a horse, aren't you?"

Me: "Sorry to disappoint you, girl. I am not."

Olivia: "He's being very modest right now. His cock is as long as my forearm. I'm sure Vivian has seen it protruding through your pants from time to time."

Me: "It is not, honey. You're exaggerating. It only looks big to you because you've never taken dick before you met me."

Olivia: "It most certainly is, baby. That's why I have to use two hands to stroke you off."

Vivian: "Well, that would definitely explain all the painful moaning and squealing." We laughed.

We were looking at all the fields and farmhouses lightly covered in snow. A lot of those old farmhouses were absolutely beautiful and meticulously maintained throughout the years. This was peaceful living at its best. We never heard sirens, or domestic disputes, or any annoying sounds that city life created. I took a few sips of whiskey and the ladies wanted to try some. When they first took a swig, their faces cringed, but they didn't spit it out. We walked for about forty-five minutes, then took a smoke break. Of course, I had to take a few more shots of whiskey, as did the ladies. After a while we were all buzzing from the alcohol. We weren't slurring our words, or walking crooked, but we did feel a little *"happier"* if you know what I mean. As we all know, sometimes when we drink, we get a little brave and frisky. We say things that we would normally never say out loud. It hadn't got to that point yet, but...

Vivian: "This really isn't bad tasting whiskey. My whole body's warm and cozy. It's quite ironic that I bartend part time, and yet this is the first time I've tasted Southern Comfort."

Olivia: "Julian and I just love walking these roads from time to time. I don't care what we do, or where we go, as long as I'm with my handsome man, holding his hand."

Vivian: "Wow, girl, your engagement ring is really sparkling from the sun. That's definitely ***not*** a cubic zirconia. I'm jealous, honey. I envy you."

Olivia: "You'll have your very own one day, girl."

Me: "You two are cast from the same mold, that's for sure."

Vivian: "I would have to agree with you on that."

Me: "Hey, hold up a second. I want to show you something."

Vivian: "***Ooh, right here and now? Show me, baby!*** Let me see what makes Olivia squeal every night."

Olivia: "She's something else, isn't she?"

Me: "Do you see that huge open field over there right before the tree line?"

Olivia: "Yes, we see it."

Me: "There is going to be a gigantic senior living facility built there within the next two years. Guess who landed the contract to build it?"

Olivia: "Don't tell me a bunch of hackers landed that job."

Me: "Nope, yours truly got it. My estimate was accepted."

Olivia: "Oh, honey, that's ***great*** news for us. The master, building more happy homes. I am so proud of you, baby. Give me those lips. ***Ooh, yeah!*** "

Vivian: "I'm feeling a bit slighted here. You don't want me to feel left out, do you?" We laughed.

Me: "Of course not. Pucker up, Sexy Red."

We took a walk down that open field to where that senior facility was going to be built. I know the man who owns this acreage, so I wasn't worried about trespassing. Knowing him definitely helped in my landing that huge project. Way down towards the end of the field was an old decrepit farmhouse. We decided to go check it out and have a look around, being very cautious where we were stepping. I'll bet this old house has a lot of stories to tell.

Olivia: "I hope this place isn't haunted. Julian, don't you dare let go of me, please. If you do, then I'm heading towards the door. This place gives me the creeps."

Vivian: "Umm, yeah, I'm with her." She tightened her grip on my hand.

Me: "It is not haunted, babe. It's just an old farmhouse that has seen better days. Judging by the looks of it, I would say it was built well over a hundred years ago. If only these walls could talk."

Vivian: "If these walls start talking, I'm out of here." We laughed.

Olivia: "All the rooms are huge, honey. It seems out of place, being in the middle of a field."

Me: "These old houses have so much character. This is one of the bigger farmhouses around."

Vivian: "Honey, where's that whiskey? I need a shot or two. I have to warm my bones up again. I'm feeling a little chilly."

Olivia: "Umm, actually, I have quite the buzz from what I've drank so far. If I have any more, you'll have to drag me home."

Me: "I'm sure a lot of beautiful memories took place in this old house. I'd like to give it one more before they tear it down."

Olivia: "Ooh, what did you have in mind, baby?"

Vivian: "Yeah, I'm kind of curious myself."

I grabbed Olivia, held her up against the wall, and started kissing her. We were really getting into it after a few seconds. I knew she loved to kiss, and she was very good at it. I held her arms up over her head and started sucking on her neck until I left a couple of "*love marks*" on it. I unzipped her jacket and started feeling her beautiful breasts. Vivian just looked on, feeling left out, and wondered if she might be in on the action. I unbuttoned and unzipped Olivia's pants and stuck my hand inside her panties. This got her moaning very quietly, but very noticeably. I was using my fingers to get her very wet and horny, which she became, very quickly.

Vivian was really feeling like an outcast at this point, so she lit up a smoke and watched me and Olivia swap tongues, almost feeling rejected. Within five minutes of me putting my fingers down Olivia's pants, her body started to quiver and shake as she squirted all over my fingers, soaking her panties and causing her to let off a few very loud moans. This was getting Vivian very hot and bothered, so she finished her smoke and then pushed me up against the wall and jammed her tongue in my mouth, forcing me to take it in. That is exactly what I wanted to happen. I've kissed Vivian before, and she is a great kisser. She knows how to use that tongue. It was actually turning Olivia on watching me and Vivian get heavily into it. Vivian undid her pants for me, so I stuck my hand inside them, but not the same hand I used on Olivia. Vivian was quite a bit moister than Olivia, and that really turned me on.

As Vivian and I were kissing and sucking on each other's necks, Olivia unzipped my pants and pulled them down far enough to grab my cock, which was extremely hard at this point. She was giving me a hand job as Vivian, and I kept kissing. I left a couple of "*love marks*" on Vivian's neck as well. I had Vivian very close to squirting; I could tell by the way she was moving her body. Her pants dropped to the floor, so I pulled her panties down. I was rubbing her peach and swirling my finger around her clit ring until she squirted cum almost to the other side of the room. She was squirting like a fountain.

Now that I got both of them off, they both pinned me up against the wall, taking turns kissing me while both of them now had a hand on my cock, trying to get me to cum. Vivian was sucking on one side of my neck, while Olivia was sucking on the other side. Vivian was teasing the head of my cock with her thumb while Olivia jerked me off. I shot out chunks of cum all over Vivian's hand and then Olivia's. They both kept jerking me off until I shot another load on the floor. Afterwards, they both sucked on their fingers.

Vivian: "***Ooh, there it is, baby. Yes!*** "

Olivia: "Nice job, girl. ***Look at all that cum!*** "

Vivian: "Ten inches of cock, stroked completely dry. ***Damn, baby!*** I can see why Olivia struggles with it."

Me: "That felt amazing. Thank you both so much."

Olivia: "No, thank ***you***, sweetheart. That was ***so fucking erotic!*** Now I need a smoke."

Vivian: "That was ***fucking hot!*** And now this house has one more story to tell." She chuckled.

We kissed for a few more minutes, and then decided to head back home. We finished off the rest of the whiskey. Of course, on the way home we just had to talk about what we just did together.

Vivian: "I really can't believe what just happened." As she smiled.

Olivia: "Oh, you can certainly believe it, girl. It really happened."

Me: "It would have never happened if I didn't initiate it, so I hope neither of you have any regrets about it. I just couldn't hold back any longer."

Olivia: "Sweetheart, it's all good. It's not like we don't love each other, because we obviously do. Vivian, what are your thoughts on it? Or maybe we should talk about this once we've sobered up a bit."

Vivian: "I fucking loved it. I would do it again, even if I was completely sober."

Olivia: "In all honesty, I've very glad it happened. It was just a matter of time before it did anyways. Am I right, honey?"

Me: "You are absolutely right. I'm so glad that we got to experience that with her. We both adore you, Vivian. You know that, right?"

Vivian: "I do, honey, and I adore both of you so much. Shit... why am I sugar coating this? I have fallen deeply in love with both of you. Maybe you've picked up on that, or maybe you haven't. So, now you both know how I feel."

Olivia: "Trust me, girl, the feelings are mutual. So, are you glad that you came back?"

Vivian: "I'm happier than I've ever been in my life. So, yes, I'm ***very*** glad that I came back. It's time to start a new chapter in my life, a chapter that I hope will last forever and ever."

Olivia: "Honey, I don't remember walking this far from the house. Are we walking in circles? Did we walk ourselves into another county?" We all laughed.

Vivian: "I don't know about walking in circles, but we're definitely walking around with soaked panties. My peach is ***still*** tingling." She chuckled.

We finally made it back home. It seemed like it took forever though. That was a very nice walk. I'm sure we'll all remember it for the rest of our lives. The ladies were still feeling a little tipsy from the whiskey, so they relaxed on the pullout sofa and watched a Christmas movie. It was still quite early, but we did drink quite a bit of whiskey during our walk. They snuggled up together under a blanket, and within a half hour, they were both sleeping. I took a few pictures of them because they did look adorable all nestled under the blanket. I probably should have joined them because I was a bit buzzed and tired myself.

While the ladies were sleeping, I decided to make Chicken French for dinner. I will let the ladies sleep for as long as they want, and when they do get up, we'll eat. They are certainly not expecting me to make our dinner, since I hardly ever cook. Forty-five minutes later, I had the Chicken French all made, keeping it warm in the oven. I also set the table and whipped up a salad to go with our dinner. Olivia woke up first and was surprised that the table was all set for dinner. She had to re-think things because she wasn't sure if she set the table before she took a nap. I poured her a cup of coffee, and we had a smoke.

Olivia: "Honey, did you do all of this? I honestly don't remember if I did it earlier. Something smells nice. What is it? Is there something in the oven?"

Me: "I made us Chicken French for dinner while you were napping."

Olivia: "Aww, baby you didn't have to do that. Thank you, sweetheart." She kisses me.

Me: "I thought that maybe you ladies would have a headache from all the whiskey you drank, so I didn't want you to have to do anything when you woke up."

Vivian finally woke up and joined us at the table. I poured her a cup of coffee, and she had a smoke with us. She saw that the table was all set.

Vivian: "Olivia, I would have helped you make dinner and set the table. I wish you had waited."

Olivia: "Actually, Julian cooked us Chicken French, and did all of this while we were napping."

Vivian: "Honey, you did this, for us?" She kisses me.

Me: "Yes, all for the Christmas cuties. Are you hungry yet?"

Vivian: "I can eat, for sure, and soak up some of the alcohol. I need some aspirin first."

Olivia: "Grab me some too, girl. I have a slight headache as well."

We ate our dinner and reflected on the wonderful Christmas we've had. We did talk more about our intense make out session in that old farmhouse. That will be talked about for quite some time, I'm sure.

Vivian: "Julian, this Chicken French is delicious. Great job on it, honey."

Olivia: "He did good, didn't he, girl? Truth be told, I wasn't in any mood to cook once I woke up, but I still would have. I'm waiting for this aspirin to start working." She chuckled.

Vivian: "Yeah, my head is pounding, but not like it was. How much did we drink? ***Shit!*** "

Me: "We drank a whole bottle of Southern Comfort, not a real big bottle though, but definitely enough. So, I have to ask you something. Now that we're not as drunk as we were, is everyone ok with what happened earlier during our walk?"

Olivia: "I am, yes. Completely ok with it. I remember it vividly."

Vivian: "I have no regrets, whatsoever, at all. ***That was hot as fuck!*** You weren't lying, girl, he's hanging pretty heavy down there." She looks at me and winks.

Me: "Well, you ***were*** kind of drunk, Vivian. Maybe you were seeing double vision." I winked at her.

Vivian: "Honeys, you do know that I have to leave in a couple of days, right? I need to get back home and take care of business, unfortunately. I will be back for your wedding; you can count on that. I wouldn't miss that for the world."

Olivia: "We know you have to go, Viv. Let's not get too emotional about it right now. Ok?"

Vivian: "Ok. But I think you should know that when I do come back, I'm never leaving again. Are you still ok with that?"

Olivia: "***Really, girl? Of course, we're ok with that!*** "

Me: "Yeah, I don't know about that. She's ***way too hot*** to have around the house."

Vivian: "You've already admitted that you love me and promised to take care of me. So, the way I see it, you're stuck with me. And if you keep being a smart ass, I will ***never*** jerk you off again." She smiled.

Olivia: "She's got you there, baby. And at this point, we couldn't stand being without you, Viv."

Me: "Ok. You can come back to stay with us, but remember what I told you about never, ever, allowing any man to put his hands on you again." We laughed.

Vivian: "I know, honey, my body and heart belong to you and Olivia. And it's all good, baby. It's all going to be ***very good***."

It was the day after Christmas, and I managed to sleep in a bit. When I got dressed and headed out to the kitchen for a cup of coffee, the ladies were sitting at the table having their coffee and a smoke.

Olivia: "Happy Birthday, sweetheart. And you thought I forgot. Didn't you?"

Vivian: "Happy Birthday, baby. We love you. This is your special day, so whatever your heart desires, we'll take care of you."

They both stood up and walked over to me, and then gave me a kiss and hug. The kisses were a little more intense than what we usually did for good morning kisses. If this is the way we're going to kiss from now on, I'm certainly ok with that.

Olivia: "My sexy man turned thirty-seven today. We're ten years apart, honey."

Me: "I don't remember even telling you when my birthday is. How did you know?"

Olivia: "That's actually quite simple. Right after I got my Blazer, you sent me to the store for something and gave me your wallet to pay for the merchandise because it had the debit card in it."

Vivian: "You can't keep anything from your ladies, honey. We'll always find out." She winked.

Me: "Well, it's just another day to me, so I never really celebrated it."

Olivia: "Well, that has changed, baby. When I turned twenty-seven earlier this year, that was the best birthday I have ever had because it was the day I met you, my love. So, around here, birthdays will always call for celebration. Mine's in January, Vivian's is in February, and yours is in December."

Me: "And? There's more to that."

Vivian: "What do you mean?"

Me: "Well, our birthdays are in three consecutive months, and all three of our birthdays are on the twenty-sixth day of those months."

Olivia: "I never thought of that. That's kind of cool, huh?"

Vivian: "That ***is*** kind of cool. Maybe it's more than just a coincidence."

Olivia: "Honey, I think the dishwasher is messed up. It's making some funky noises, and the water won't turn on. And now I can't get the door to open. Will you look at it, please? I would like to use it today."

Me: "Sure. I never used it anyways. I prefer doing the dishes by hand."

I went over to the dishwasher to see if I could get the door open. It opened right up for me, and inside it was a gift-wrapped box, obviously a birthday gift.

Me: "What is this? What did you ladies do now?"

Vivian: "Oh, you're about to find out, handsome man."

I ripped the paper off it and opened the box. In it, were two 8x10 pictures of the ladies posing with the cars. Olivia was standing by the Z/28, and Vivian was standing by the Trans Am. My heart just dropped to my feet. They were both wearing cut-off jean shorts, red and black checkered shirts, and work boots, just like Olivia wears when she helps me at work. I was on the verge of crying, and it was very hard to hold it in. I had to put my hands over my eyes because I just couldn't hold it back. The girls came over and hugged me, waiting for me to get it all out. I was very proud and fighting it with all that I had.

Me: "These are absolutely beautiful. Thank you both from the bottom of my heart. I wish I could say more, but I can't seem to get the words out right now."

Olivia: "Oh, honey, it's ok to cry, even if you're a man. Don't be proud, sweetheart. You ***know*** we won't think any less of you for showing your emotions."

Vivian: "Baby, it's perfectly fine to express how you feel. It makes you more of a man, in my opinion."

I held them both so tight and I did not want to let go. I didn't all out cry, but my eyes certainly watered, and I couldn't seem to wipe them dry fast enough.

Me: "I love you both so very much. You mean the world to me. You ***are*** my world. My life would feel so empty and meaningless without you."

Olivia: "Sweetheart, I am yours forever. You ***know*** that baby. You already know what you mean to me. You will ***never*** be without me. I swear to you."

Vivian: "I'm not going anywhere either, honey. I am in this for the long haul. I think you know that."

Me: "How did you pull this off?"

Olivia: "We just did it while you were at work one day. The keys to the cars are always hanging on the hook, so it was pretty easy. Vivian pulled the Trans Am out of the garage, and I pulled the Z/28 out."

Me: "You ladies are incredible. I just adore you. I don't know how to thank you." I kissed the pictures.

Vivian: "We've already figured that out for you. You can thank ***her*** tonight in bed, and you can thank ***me*** by giving her a good pounding, because you ***know*** I will be listening." We all laughed.

Chapter 10 – Birthday Girls and Wedding Bells

It's a brand-new year and we can only hope that this one will be better than the last, although last year was the best one for me so far because that's when I met my beautiful and precious Olivia, who was now my fiancé`. We will be getting married next month on Valentine's Day. We were both ecstatic and a little on the nervous side to be honest. Olivia's birthday is this month, on the twenty-sixth, exactly one year from the day we met. Nothing in this world will mean more to me than making her my wife, although we already live as husband and wife, and I already wear my wedding band. So, there is a lot going on for the first part of this year.

Vivian went back home shortly after Christmas, but she will be here for our wedding, and this time, she is staying with us for good. She was home tying up loose ends and getting rid of everything that she didn't need to bring with her. All she really needs is her clothes and anything personal and precious to her. Olivia and I will be married in our new home, so we have been busy making the transition over. We've been living in our new home now and are trying to get settled in. Vivian did call to tell us that she could be here within a week if we wanted her to come that early. Of course, we want her here as soon as she can get here. We've missed her like crazy. Olivia did tell her that we were now living in the new place and slowly moving things over from the old place.

I'm framing another house this week about a half hour away from my house. I really do love working close to home. I've been very fortunate to land all of the local jobs and I have plenty of work now to keep myself and my guys busy for the whole year. I don't want to accept too many more jobs because I need to be available to build that huge senior living complex. That will be an enormous job for us, but we enjoy the challenge and that's when we go into beast mode. I have a couple of new guys to help keep up with the workload. They were sent to me by a temp agency, so I will see how they work out. I only have them for six months as of right now, per contract.

Olivia: "Honey, when Vivian gets here, will she be living in our old place, or will she be here with us? We haven't really talked about that in detail."

Me: "Well, do you think that she would feel comfortable living there all by herself, or will it be too much for her? I certainly don't want to overwhelm her or have her being scared there all alone."

Olivia: "Sweetheart, you know damn well that you don't want her staying in the old house by herself, as much as I don't. There's no way we can even bare not having her here with us at this point."

Me: "I know, honey. Trust me, she will be right here with us from day one. I'm not sure she even knows that yet. I think she's under the impression that she'll be staying all alone in the other house. She hasn't flat out told me that she didn't want to stay there."

Olivia: "Speaking of Vivian, she's calling me right now. Should I put her on the speaker phone?"

Me: "Yeah, you should do that."

Olivia: "Hi girl, how are you doing? Everything ok there?"

Vivian: "Hi, Olivia, I miss you guys so much. I want to come back, right now." She chuckled.

Me: "Hello, Sexy Red. So, what's going on with you? Are you coming back home to stay?"

Vivian: "Hi, Julian. I didn't realize I was on the speaker phone. Umm, honey, I need to talk with you about something and I don't want it to come out wrong."

Me: "What's wrong, girl? Are you not coming?"

Vivian: "OK, I'm going to lay this all out right now. I think you both know what you mean to me, and I don't ever want to be without you. I'm feeling like you both love me more than I have ever been loved in my life, and I cherish that special love between us."

Olivia: "Vivian, you have to know by now just how much you mean to us. We love you very deeply and adamantly."

Vivian: "I do know that. That's what gets me through these days. It's your love that pulls me through and gives me the strength to carry on. I am so in love with you, and I want to spend the rest of my life with you. In all honesty, it really scares me a little to be living in your old house by myself. I do have insecurities that I deal with. I want to be with you, and I want to be close to you, so I will stay in the old place, just to have you both in my life, but it's not my preference."

Me: "Well, what ***is*** your preference, girl? Do you want to live with us in the new house and have your own huge bedroom?"

Vivian: "Yes. Can I, please? Do you love me enough to do that for me?"

Me: "Of course I love you enough to do that for you. And for the record, I was ***never*** going to let you live there by yourself anyways."

Olivia: "See, Vivian, he does love you, more than you know."

Vivian: "Thank you both so much. So, you ***were*** serious about taking care of me. I don't know how I could ever re-pay you both for opening your hearts to me."

Me: "Say it, Olivia."

Olivia: "There will be no re-paying in this house. Everything we do for you is out of deep love and respect for you."

We heard Vivian starting to sniffle a little because the sad world she had been living in would no longer exist, and she was about to be part of the most beautiful love and world she had ever imagined.

Vivian: "Umm, I need your undivided attention for a minute, please."

Olivia: "Yes, girl, what is it?"

Vivian: "My car is packed and I'm on my way to be with you. I will be there in four hours if that works for you. I know it's very short notice."

Olivia and I both let out a huge sigh of relief, knowing that Vivian was coming back for good.

Me: "That's the best news I've heard all day. Drive safe, girl. Our arms are open wide, waiting for you."

Olivia: "We can't wait to see you too. Come home, honey. Let us take care of you."

Vivian got in her car and headed home to us, never looking back in the rear-view mirror. Olivia and I just snuggled up on the couch, watching the clock, waiting for her to arrive.

Olivia: "Honey, you know it means a lot to Vivian that we care so much about her. She's leaving her friends, her job, and her entire world behind just to be part of our lives."

Me: "I know she is. It didn't sound to me like she was living a very happy life wherever she was anyway. I'm very flattered that she loves us so much. I mean, I could see her loving you because you two have a history together, an unfinished love."

Olivia: "You honestly don't know why she loves you, baby? She loves you for the same reasons I love you, only ***our love*** is on another level. Vivian is not like other women, just as I am not. We both have our own reasons for loving her, sweetheart."

Me: "All I know is that I have this deep passion to love her and make sure she's able to live the life she has always wanted to live. You know me better than anyone, honey. I ***don't*** just love anybody."

Olivia: "I know you don't. That's why Vivian and I feel so blessed and fortunate to have your love. With that being said, you also know that she and I love you from the very bottoms of our hearts. We both know exactly what we mean to you. You've already proved that to us."

Me: "I swear to you, honey, I will be the best husband I can possibly be to you. And you know me well enough to know that I only say what I mean."

Several hours later, we heard Vivian pull in the driveway. When Vivian got out of her car, she walked very quickly towards us and latched on to us.

Olivia: "Oh yes, our sweet Vivian. Welcome home, honey."

Vivian: "I never wanted to leave in the first place. I just had a bunch of shit to deal with before I could start a new life." She started crying.

Me: "That's all behind you, girl. You are finally at your calling. Welcome to our twisted world. I made sure that the bed had new sheets on it, and there was plenty of food to eat. I will keep the utilities in my name for now, but eventually you'll have to put them all in your name. I kept the cable on for you too. Olivia gave it a good cleaning for you, so it's all good to go."

Vivian: "What? The old place? But I thought…"

Me: "The old place, it's all set up for you." Vivian looked puzzled.

Olivia: "He's only fucking with you, honey."

Vivian: "Julian, I love you, ***but I will beat your ass!*** That wasn't funny, ***honey!*** "

Me: "I'm sorry, girl. Why don't you ladies go in the house and open a bottle of wine, and I'll unload the car. I'm sure Vivian needs something to calm her nerves."

Vivian: "Wait. Not yet. I need to do two things right now. The first thing is to tell you both how much I love and adore you. And the second thing is, all I thought about as I was driving here, was how amazing your kisses felt. So, I ***really*** need some of that tongue. I am ***so fucking horny right now!*** "

We actually kissed several times. Olivia and I were taking turns with her, but it was just kissing, nothing else, although at one point I almost laid her on the hood of her car and ripped her pants off.

Olivia: "Are you ready for that glass of wine yet?" We laughed.

Vivian: "I sure am. It's good to be home. And I am never leaving again, ever."

Me: "Can you promise us that you will never leave?"

Vivian: "Oh yes. I can promise you that, just like you promised to take care of me and be the only man in my life. That's our deal, and we only say what we mean. Right?"

Olivia: "She's sounding more and more like you every day, sweetheart." We laughed.

Vivian: "Olivia, we need to go shopping for wedding dresses very soon. But I hope not tonight because I just want to get drunk and hang out with the two most important people in my life."

Me: "Well, we are very flattered that you see us in that way."

Vivian: "I was talking about Olivia and my ten-inch strap-on." We all laughed so hard.

Me: "Go to your room right now, young lady, and don't come out until I come and get you."

Vivian: "***Ooh, are you going to spank my ass?*** You ***want*** this ass, and you know it, Julian."

Olivia: "Oh, be careful what you say to him, girl. You've seen his cock, so you better be damn sure that you want it in your ass."

Vivian: "Oh, I've seen his cock, honey. It would give my biggest dildo a run for the money."

It may seem like the way Vivian talks to Olivia and me, that she is going to be nothing more than our live-in *"fuck buddy."* That is just the way we talk to each other. That whole scene in the old farmhouse was mainly due to all the alcohol we had in our systems, even though after the fact, we all loved that it happened and had no regrets. Me and Olivia will always make Vivian feel that she is loved, accepted, cared for, and adored by us. If that involves a little intense kissing from time to time, then I see that as being innocent foreplay. Whether or not that changes into something more intimate, is something that time will tell us. We're just glad that she's here with us. We're obviously all branches from the same tree.

Vivian: "Umm, Julian, we haven't talked about how much rent I need to pay you for staying here. I do have some money saved up so I could pay you for the next few months."

Me: "I didn't charge Olivia any rent to stay in the old place before we became involved, and I'm sure as hell not going to charge ***you*** anything either."

Vivian: "But I have to pay you something or else I'll feel like a freeloader, and I don't want that on my conscience. And I will look for a job starting tomorrow."

Me: "Vivian, you are not paying us any rent, ever. This is your place as much as it is mine and Olivia's. I built this house in my dreams, and in my dreams, no one pays to live here. This house has already been paid for. All you need to do is help Olivia out with cleaning, laundry, grocery shopping, and whatever else she needs you for. So, as of now, you are officially our sexy live-in maid."

Olivia: "The man of the house has spoken, girl. Just relax, enjoy your life, and enjoy this beautiful house with us. There is nothing but deep love inside these walls. You will feel it soon enough."

Vivian: "I don't know what to say to that. I feel like crying again because I'm finally happy."

Me: "As far as your feeling like you have to get a job; you don't have to. You can help Olivia out once we turn one of the extra rooms into an office for my business. You can help her run the day-to-day operations. Does that interest you at all?"

Vivian: "That sounds amazing and fun, working from home. I love it already."

Me: "Well, first you'll have to fill out an application and ace the job interview. If all that pans out, then you'll get a call from us, setting up a second interview."

Vivian: "***Julian, you're fucking with me right now, aren't you?*** "

Me: "No. I'm just following the company protocol."

Vivian: "You know, you're the reason why I drink so much damn wine." Olivia and I laughed.

Olivia: "Girl, he's just being a smart ass, as usual. He's obviously flirting with you, so he must like you."

Vivian: "***Oh yeah? Well, he just blew any chance he ever had of taking me and my sweet ass to bed!*** "

I loved messing with Vivian. She has a very unique sense of humor. I adored her so much that I liked to get her going at times. I still had a lot of unpacking to do. I haven't started setting up my music room yet. Everything was still in boxes. I was in no hurry at this point. I was just glad that we moved everything over from the other house. If I do decide to sell the other house, it will be sold completely furnished. I may just decide to rent it out, that was still up in the air. Olivia and I will talk more about it very soon. I include her in all my decisions. The only things left over at the other house were the cars, which I wanted to drive over very soon.

I called my friend Eric to see if he wanted to bring his wife and kids over to have pizza and wings and hang out, but I got his voice mail. I would actually consider him to be my best friend. He's been working for me for seven years now and he runs the show when I'm out bidding on other jobs. He helped me build the garage and deck at my other place. Eric did call me back to say that he and his wife and kids were going to his in- laws for the night but would love to get together very soon.

Olivia helped Vivian set up her new bedroom, which she absolutely loved. She was so happy being back here with us that she had a certain glow to her. It really melts my heart to see those two beautiful ladies always happy and smiling. I was very honored and proud to love them. I had the two pictures in my hand that they made for me, the ones with them standing next to the cars.

Me: “Hey Olivia and Vivian, could you please come here for a minute?”

Olivia: “Sure, what’s up, my love? Hold on, Vivian’s doing something really quick. We’ll be right down.”

They both came downstairs and saw me standing in the kitchen holding something behind my back. So, naturally they wondered what it was.

Olivia: “Here we are, honey. Did you need something?”

Me: “I just want to thank you both again from the bottom of my heart for these very stunning pictures. You two are by far the most beautiful and sexiest women I have ever laid my eyes on, and I love you both more than you will ever know. That’s it. That’s all I wanted to say.”

Olivia: “Baby, you mean the world to me, and I’m quite sure Vivian feels the same way. We love you.”

Vivian: “She’s right, Julian, we love you more than ***you*** will ever know. I can’t wait to see you two get married. It will be my pleasure to give my best friend away to the most amazing man I have ever known. One day, I want to have the same love that you two have for each other.”

Me: “Vivian, you already had it the moment you came back to us.”

Olivia: "Oh, honey, I just adore the man that you are. Thank you for loving ***my*** best friend."

Once the ladies finished setting up Vivian's room, they came downstairs, and we all got cozy on the pullout sofa. We actually found a movie that we liked and watched the whole thing without falling asleep or making out. Me and Olivia had a tendency to do that. We tried to keep our making out behind closed doors so Vivian wouldn't feel left out or slighted.

Me: "Someone has a birthday coming up, Ms. Olivia."

Olivia: "Someone also has a one-year anniversary coming up, Mr. Julian."

Me: "That's right, and Vivian's birthday is coming up next month, so I have to tell you both something, and please don't get mad at me."

Vivian: "What did you do ***now***, Julian?"

Me: "Well, I sort of booked you both a weekend spa getaway for two days. It's my birthday gift to both of you. Are you ok with that?"

Olivia: "***You did?*** "

Vivian: "Please tell us that you're being serious right now. Because I never know with you."

Me: "I am very serious. You ladies leave out Friday morning and you come back Sunday morning."

Olivia: "Where is it at, sweetheart? Close by, I hope."

Me: "It's about a forty-five-minute drive from here. The place is very nice, and it has already been paid for, so go and have a good time and enjoy the massages."

Olivia: "Aww, thank you, baby, so much." We kissed.

Vivian: "Yes, thank you, honey. You certainly know how to take care of us. What a very pleasant surprise. That certainly deserves a kiss."

Olivia: "Once I get done kissing him, you two can have at it all you want."

Vivian: "Be careful what you say, Olivia. Remember, I've been ***a little*** on the horny side lately."

Me: "I just figured with the wedding coming up quickly, and your birthdays, it would be best to send you away for the weekend beforehand."

It was Friday morning, and the ladies were getting ready to leave for the weekend. I was heading to work right after I sent them off. It was going to feel very weird not having them around for the weekend, but they were very excited about it, and I was glad to do that for them. This will be the first time that Olivia and I will be apart since we've met.

Olivia: "Honey, why can't you come with us? I don't want to be away from you all weekend. I'm going to get separation anxiety."

Me: "You'll be fine. You have Vivian to hang out with, and you ***know*** she will be fun."

Vivian: "Umm, are you insinuating that I'm a troublemaker?"

Me: "No. Not at all." I rolled my eyes.

Vivian: "Keep it up, honey. You'll never kiss these lips again."

Me: "Make sure you call me when you get there, and please drive safely. Know that I love you."

Olivia: "We love you, too, sweetheart. I will not stop thinking about you."

They headed out, and I headed off to work. I had to finish up on my current job so I could start another one. I was in for a long day, but I am like an energy ball once I get going. That may explain why I only get four or five hours of sleep a night. I'm wired to stay up late and get up early. I love to be awake when everyone else is sleeping. I've spent many nights just sitting on the deck and staring off into the sky, hoping to see shooting stars or something bizarre up there. I'm actually thinking about investing in a telescope. I could have a lot of fun with that. I don't know how you feel about other civilizations occupying planets, but Olivia and I firmly believe that there are other beings out there.

I have been wanting to get two puppies now that we've moved into the new house. I purposely built an extra room just for them. I haven't told Olivia yet and won't mention it until after we're married. It will be part of a wedding present to her. I've always loved dogs, but I do love animals in general. I donate every month to animal shelters. I want to get two lab/shepherd mixes, one boy, and one girl. I already have their names picked out. About an hour after I got to work, Olivia called me to say that they were there safely. She put me on the speaker phone.

Olivia: "Hi, baby, I love you. Umm, you are just full of surprises, aren't you?"

Me: "Hello, girl. And what do you mean about surprises?"

Vivian: "She's talking about these gorgeous roses that were on our nightstands when we got to our room. Do you know anything about that?"

Olivia: "Yeah, honey, are those part of the weekend package?"

Me: "I had those delivered there just for you. I hope you like them. The white ones are for you and the red are for Vivian. I know how much you love white roses."

Vivian: "Thank you, baby. I love them."

Me: "You are both quite welcome. I hope you enjoy the pool and the sauna while you're there. I'll be putting in a very long day today, finishing this house up."

Olivia: "Oh, we'll definitely be hitting the sauna, for sure. Well, I won't hold you up, baby. I know you're working. I love you so much, sweetheart and can't wait to come back home to you."

Me: "Call me whenever you want and have a great time. I love you, Olivia. You too, Vivian."

I put in a fourteen-hour workday and came home. I wasn't exactly fond of walking into a quiet house. Olivia always met me at the door in her sexy maid's outfit. Vivian had followed suit and started wearing a sexy maid's outfit too. I have so many pictures of them on my phone and computer posing with those outfits on. If I ever lose my phone and someone finds it, they are going to get quite the eyeful.

I made myself a White Russian and went into my music room to play for a little while. There was no one here besides me so I cranked up the amps and let off some steam. The Les Paul that Olivia bought me is my main guitar now. I have several vintage guitars that spend their lives in the cases. I bring those out when I'm looking for a certain tone and feel. All of my amps are also vintage tube amps; back when they were built with quality in mind and not quantity. I refuse to buy any new guitar or amp. Their quality has turned into complete shit, and they're worth less than half of what people end up paying for them. Those are just my opinions, but I truly believe them to be fact.

Olivia called me before her and Vivian went to bed, thanking me again for their surprise getaway. They really do work very hard keeping our home in order. It is a lot of space to keep clean; overwhelming, I'm sure. The ladies had my office all set up and business has been very good. They both have their own desk and computer. It's a typical office setting, but on a very small scale. My company is not huge by any means; not yet. I am thinking about branching out and hiring more crews. I have turned down several huge jobs because I simply don't have the manpower. Do I want more headaches, or do I want to keep my sanity? That's the question I keep asking myself.

I worked all day Saturday just to keep up with the workload. I do have a great crew of hard-working guys. Everyone gets along great, and they are always on time. I don't have any drug users or immature assholes working for me. That will not be tolerated at all. The moment I see them playing on their cell phones when they're supposed to be working, is the moment they are clocked out for the day, and probably for good. There are rare exceptions of family emergencies, or someone's wife going into labor, but other than that, I keep things tight and efficient.

It was Sunday morning and Vivian called to tell me that they were on their way home, and from what they told me, they had had a blast. They had some stories to share with me. They're not troublemakers at all, but because they're very gorgeous women, they seem to attract a lot of attention wherever they go, and they usually dress to kill when they're out in public. I saw them pulling up in the driveway and met them there. It felt great to have them back home. We gave each other a kiss and hug, and I unloaded the car for them.

Olivia: "There's my sexy, handsome man. I've missed you, baby. That was awesome, thank you so much for that."

Me: "I'm glad you had a great time, ladies. I'm sure I'm going to get an earful, right?"

Vivian: "Yeah, something like that." She chuckled.

Me: "Are you hungry? Would you like me to make you something to eat? I just had a huge egg omelet and a half a loaf of bread for toast, so I'm full for quite a while."

Olivia: "No, sweetheart, we ate breakfast right before we left. The food was ***so*** good. I feel like I put on five pounds."

Vivian: "That must be from all the strawberries we ate. Right, girl?" She winked.

Me: "Something tells me that there's more to the story than just eating strawberries."

Vivian: "Well, it's not so much ***that*** we ate the strawberries. It's ***how*** we ate them that's interesting."

Olivia: "We won't even get into the way Vivian was eating a banana during breakfast this morning in the main dining room, in front of thirty or forty other people."

Vivian: "It's not ***my fault*** that people weren't minding their own business. I was only trying to tease that one guy who was hitting on me in the lounge last night."

Olivia: "Well, he wasn't the ***only one*** watching you suck off that banana." She chuckled.

Vivian: "I was only trying to liven the place up. Everyone looked so lethargic and depressed."

Me: "That certainly sounds like Vivian, always stirring things up."

Fast forwarding to Olivia's twenty-eighth birthday, Vivian and I got her several gift cards to her favorite stores and took her out to dinner. The ladies had already bought their matching wedding dresses, so there wasn't a whole lot to do before the wedding, which was in two weeks. I'm just wearing a pair of black dress pants, a black long sleeve button shirt, and my white suspenders. There was just going to be a handful of people here, nothing too crazy. Olivia and I hadn't talked about a honeymoon yet, and we aren't the type of people who feel like we have to go on a vacation. A lot of people love going on them, but we were not those people.

Me: "Olivia, are you sure that you don't want to invite your parents here for the wedding ceremony? I'll pay to fly them here."

Olivia: "I know you would, honey, but they're in Russia visiting their families right now. They usually stay for quite a while when they go."

Me: "I just don't want them getting mad that we didn't invite them to their daughter's wedding."

Olivia: "I've already explained to them that it's just going to a very small ceremony right here in our living room. They're not upset, honest. We can have them over at a later date."

Vivian: "Julian, did you know that Olivia looks ***exactly*** like her mother? Just a younger version of her. Nikki is gorgeous. She's definitely a hot MILF."

Me: "She didn't tell me that she looked exactly like her, but she did say that her mother was very beautiful. I can't wait to meet her parents. I've heard a lot about them."

Vivian: "Nikki and I always got along great. I would love to see her again."

Olivia: "We will wait until they're back from their trip, and then I'll invite them here for a few days. I'm sure they'd love to come."

Me: "That's fine, honey. I'm glad they're not mad. I really want them to like me."

Ok, so it was now Valentine's Day, and the day that Olivia and I are getting married. I was up very early this morning. The ladies were still sleeping, and I wanted to make sure that everything was all set for the ceremony. I didn't want Olivia and Vivian to stress over cooking anything, so we decided to keep it very simple and just have a couple of sheet pizzas delivered and a bunch of chicken wings. A few of my workers will be here, as will my friend Lena, who records wedding receptions and handles all of the pictures. We will be married at 1:00 p.m. this afternoon, so I'm expecting everyone to be here by noon, except the pastor, who will be here right before the ceremony. My sweet Olivia was going to be plenty nervous today, I'm sure. I was actually quite nervous myself, to be honest. I had never been married before either, so we were both going to be dealing with a new set of chills.

It was around 10:00 a.m. now and the ladies finally rolled out of bed. I was sitting at the table having a smoke and a cup of coffee. On the center island in the kitchen were two vases with roses in them, the white ones were for Olivia and the red ones, for Vivian, just like the ones they got on their weekend getaway. There were also two boxes of chocolates, two cards, and a small box taped to each card. I bought both of them matching diamond necklaces and bracelets. Olivia came over to me, sat on my lap, and then Vivian came over and sat on my other lap.

Olivia: "Good morning, baby, I love you with all my heart. Today's our day, sweetheart; the day I've waited for my whole life."

Me: "I have too, honey. Today you will officially be Mrs. Olivia Castle, and I couldn't be happier and prouder. You are going to be the sexiest, most beautiful bride, ever. Vivian, you will be the hottest and sexiest maid of honor that ever existed."

Vivian: "Aww, thank you, baby, I love you, Julian."

Olivia: "Oh, more roses for us? Honey, you are too much. I just love white roses."

Vivian: "These are so beautiful, honey. Thank you, sexy man."

They got off my lap, went over and smelled their roses, read their cards, and opened their boxes. The sun was shining clearly through the huge windows, and as soon as they took their necklaces and bracelets out of the box, they were sparkling beautifully. Olivia started crying her eyes out. Vivian was in tears too, but she was able to hold them back better than Olivia.

Olivia: "I hope I have enough strength in me to make it through this day. You are my everything, Julian."

Me: "As you are mine. Is it too early to start drinking?"

Vivian: "I'm starting right after I finish this cup of coffee. She chuckled.

We all sat at the table and were having our coffee and a smoke. Olivia was sitting on my lap again. She was only wearing her short, silky robe with no panties or bra on. I was holding back the urge to squeeze her tits as we were talking, which was very hard because her nipples were protruding through her robe.

Vivian: "It's your day, girl. I'm so happy for you. I love you so much. I'm very excited for you. You've waited your whole life for this."

Olivia: "Thank you, girl. I love you too, you know that. I'm going to need both of you to help get me through this day. I'm already a nervous wreck."

It was getting close to 12:00 p.m. so the ladies drank a quick glass of wine, and then headed to take their showers. Vivian showered downstairs, and Olivia was in the master bedroom shower. I joined Olivia as she was taking hers. I couldn't resist the urge to slip inside her for a few minutes. I woke up extremely horny this morning. The next time we have sex, it will be as husband and wife.

I was showered, dressed, and ready in less than twenty minutes, which was a good thing, because Eric and Becky arrived just as I was walking downstairs. Shortly after that, Lena arrived, as well as Dave, Mike and Greg, my employees. Lena started recording as soon as she got here. We all sat at the bar in my basement, having drinks and shooting the shit. At 12:45 p.m. the pastor showed up, so we all headed upstairs into the living room, waiting for Olivia and Vivian to finish getting ready. They were still upstairs in the bathroom. Vivian yelled down the stairs.

Vivian: "Are you ready for us, honey? Can we come down now?"

Me: "You sure can."

They came strutting down the stairs wearing these gorgeous silk evening dresses. Olivia's was white, while Vivian's was red. Their hair was pulled back behind their ears. They looked absolutely stunning, and I was finding it very hard to react to what I was seeing. They were both wearing the necklace and bracelet that I had just got them. I made sure that Lena captured them coming down the stairs. Me and the guys were in complete awe. I'm sure as the guys were watching this, they wondered who the hot ass redhead was with Olivia. No one had met her yet, so obviously no one knew that she lived with us. And furthermore, they had no idea about our relationship with Vivian.

Eric: "Bro, you are one lucky man. You have one very beautiful lady there. I can't believe you're finally getting married."

Me: "Thank you, brother. I ***am*** very fortunate."

Pastor: "Shall we get started?"

Olivia and I were standing in front of the pastor holding hands. She was squeezing my hand very tight. Eric was next to me, and Vivian was next to Olivia. I won't go into the whole ceremonial dialogue. I'll just get to the part where we said, *"I do"* and kissed for the first time as husband and wife. Olivia and Vivian started crying but tried to keep their composure. Everyone was giving us hugs and congratulating us. Lena recorded everything and took a lot of pictures. She basically put the recorder on a tripod as she was snapping off her camera. We all wandered back to the bar area where Eric was playing bartender.

Eric: "I would like to propose a toast to the best boss and best friend a guy could have. Congratulations to both of you. Olivia, you look very beautiful. You're both very lucky and fortunate to have each other. Here's to a lifetime of love and happiness."

Olivia: "Thank you, Eric, for being such a great friend."

Me: "***Shit, I forgot!*** Everyone, this gorgeous redheaded bombshell is Vivian. She's Olivia's best friend, and also our new live-in maid. I apologize for not introducing you to each other earlier. I've had a lot on my mind today."

Becky: "You live here with them, Vivian? Wow, that's cool."

Vivian: "I do, yes. I'm the new maid. I help Olivia out around the house, and also in the office for Julian's business."

Eric: "Honey, why can't ***we*** get a maid?" We all laughed.

Dave: "That may be dangerous to your health, dude."

Becky: "You aren't kidding there, Dave. If he's not careful, he's going to be sleeping in the doghouse tonight all by himself."

Vivian: "I would like to propose a toast too. Olivia, you're my girl, and I love you. I'm so glad that you've found true, deep love and happiness. You deserve it. Julian, I've told you before, but I'll say it again; thank you so much for taking care of and loving my best friend. I love you both, you know that. It's an honor to know both of you."

Me: "Thank you, Vivian, and thank you to everyone for sharing this special day with us. Olivia, you are the most beautiful lady I have ever met in my life. That's not the only reason why I married you. You're also the warmest, most loving, compassionate and selfless person I know. You ***know*** that my heart belongs to you. I will love you beyond forever."

Olivia: "Julian, you are my man in full, and you are every bit as beautiful as I pictured you in my dreams. I am so proud and honored to be your wife. Thank you for taking such great care of me and loving me the way you do. You have ***my*** heart forever, baby, beyond forever. Thank you for creating this beautiful world for me, for us. I love you so much, beyond words, and beyond forever." She started crying.

Now that all of the toasts were done, we could get down to some serious drinking and celebrating. The pizza and wings arrived, and we all dug in. The pastor had to leave, so I showed him out and thanked him for his service. We started a pool tournament, and I even fired up the hot tub in case anyone felt the need to get in. I don't play pool very often, I'm horrible at it, but our sweet Vivian turned out to be quite the player. I would say that within two hours everyone had a bit of a buzz going. Mike, Greg, and Dave can really pound the booze. After Lena took more pictures, we told her to set down the camera and join in on the fun. There's no reason why she should be left out of all the partying.

Me: "Olivia, you look absolutely vibrant today. That dress you have on is way beyond sexy, and you wear it very well. Have I told you lately how incredibly sexy and beautiful you are?"

Olivia: "Oh, honey, you look so fucking hot all dressed up like that. Damn, I can't wait to get you into bed and ride your cock all night. I'm going to fuck ***you*** sore this time." She chuckled.

Me: "Do you want me to tell everyone to leave?" She laughed.

All of the ladies went into the hot tub. Between Vivian's and Olivia's wardrobe, they found swimsuits to fit the other ladies. They were all drinking champagne and having a blast. Olivia kept staring at her diamond ring and wedding band. The ladies got a little looser with their vocabulary now that they were chugging champagne and wine.

Lena: "So, Vivian, do you have a special man in your life?"

Vivian: "I do, yes. He's also a carpenter, like Julian."

Lena: "He couldn't make it today? That's too bad."

Vivian: "Oh, he'll show his face sooner or later." She chuckles.

Becky: "Vivian, I love your tattoos. The nose rings look good on you and Olivia."

Olivia: "Yeah, me and Vivian have a lot in common, actually."

Vivian: "This hot tub feels amazing on my body. I may sleep in here tonight. Maybe I should grab a pillow right now while I'm thinking of it."

Me and the guys hung out at the bar and talked about guy shit. They were asking about Vivian, and how she came to be here with us. I tried to explain it the best I could without going into too much detail. The guys tried to pry more out of me than what I was telling them, but there are certain things that I just won't tell anyone. We were all feeling fine and listening to the tunes playing in the background. I had put up those two pictures of the ladies with the cars, behind the bar, and we were commenting on them.

Eric: "Damn bro, I don't know what looks hotter; the car or Vivian. How do you keep your bearings with her walking around here all day?"

Dave: "That's probably why he comes to work every day in a great mood. ***I know that I would!*** "

Mike: "I never realized how fucking big this place really is. ***Damn, we do good work!*** "

The music was loud enough that the ladies couldn't hear us talking at the bar. That was probably a good thing. We tend to get carried away when we talk, especially if it's about women. I kept looking over at the hot tub at my precious Olivia, she was absolutely glowing. It was the best Valentine's Day, ever. I was happier than I had ever been in my life. I'm sure Olivia felt the same way. The guys were getting quite drunk, and I told them that they were more than welcome to crash here tonight if they didn't want to drive home. I told the same thing to Lena, but she assured me that all she needed was a cup of coffee, and she would be fine.

I didn't expect the party to go on as long as it did. I figured that we would just have a few drinks after the ceremony to celebrate a little, maybe two or three hours at best. I also thought that the guys would want to get back home to spend time with their wives, since it was Valentine's Day. I didn't know if they had plans to go out for dinner. I was actually quite surprised that the only guy who brought his wife was Eric. We drank a lot of alcohol in a very short period of time.

After we had more pizza and wings, our guests decided to head home while they could still see straight. I had a good buzz going and I could tell that Vivian and Olivia did too, just by looking at them. We started winding down and sat at the dining room table drinking coffee and smoking. That was a very nice ceremony, and I'm glad we got to share it with a few close friends. We could have made our wedding a huge deal, but we liked to keep things simple. I left out a lot of close friends, but we would get to see each other this summer at one of my pool parties. Olivia and Vivian changed into more casual clothes, but as always, they were wearing something sexy.

Olivia: "Honey, please don't be mad at me if I fall asleep tonight while we're making love. I'm feeling a little tipsy, this coffee isn't helping. Vivian, maybe you'll be the next one getting married."

Vivian: "I don't see how, considering the only man I love just got married today, to you. You are both very fortunate to have found each other."

Olivia: "We'll see what the future brings for you, honey. Julian, can we take the Z/28 for a ride?"

Me: "No honey. We've all been drinking, and you know that I only bring it out when the weather is nice. Don't worry, honey, Spring will be here before we know it, and we'll be driving the cars again."

Olivia: "I can't wait. I also can't wait to start using the pool. Vivian, are you excited to go skinny dipping?"

Vivian: "I sure am, girl. I love to swim, especially naked." She chuckled.

Me: "Well, that's an interesting visual. I'll open the pool up right now if you ladies go skinny dipping. That cold water will wake you both up in a heartbeat."

Vivian: "Ok, now you're teasing us, honey."

Olivia: "We'll have to settle for the hot tub for now. We can still skinny dip in the hot tub, you know. It's not like there's anyone around who can see us."

Vivian: "Actually, now that everyone's gone, that's ***exactly*** what I'm doing. Are you coming, girl?"

Olivia: "I sure am, but I'm not drinking anything but water for the rest of the day. Honey, are you going to join us?"

Me: "Sure, why not, right after I make myself a White Russian."

Olivia: "You have ***all*** the White Russian you'll ***ever need*** right here, baby." She winked.

Before the ladies and I got in the hot tub, I was taking a bunch of pictures of them completely naked and even got out my camcorder. Since they had been drinking and were feeling "*happy*," they got a little daring with their poses. They were kissing a lot, and I could tell that Vivian really wanted to get a little feisty with her hands. She kept grabbing Olivia's ass and squeezing it. Olivia was showing no resistance.

Me: "Oh, my sweet, sexy Russian bride. You are the hottest ever, baby. This is the best day of my life."

Olivia: "Vivian's no slouch either, huh, baby?"

Me: "Vivian is smoking hot, that's for ***damn sure***. Sexiest maid of honor, ever."

Vivian: "Your words are very flattering, honey."

Olivia: "***Damn, Viv!*** Your peach is so wide and gaping. Did your toys stretch you out like that?"

Vivian: "I'm sure they had a lot to do with it." She chuckled.

Olivia: "Mine's finally starting to open up a bit. But I'm sure Vivian is way deeper than me."

Vivian: "I ***am*** very curious, Olivia. Are you able to take all of his cock yet?"

Olivia: "Umm***...no!*** Do you think that ***you*** could?"

Vivian: "I don't know. Maybe. Are you ever going to let me find out?" She winks.

Olivia: "You know what? We need to bring this conversation into the bedroom."

Me: "Are you sure, honey? Is that the alcohol talking, or are you really wanting this to happen?"

Olivia: "***Oh, yeah!*** I cannot resist her any longer. Can you honestly tell me right now that ***you*** don't want to bed her down too?"

Me: "Honestly, if you must know, I have fantasized about this for quite a while now. There, I said it."

Vivian: "***Ooh, fuck yeah!*** This is going to work out great for me because I was actually going to try my luck at persuading you both into my bedroom. After all, that ***is*** where your wedding gift is."

Olivia: "It is, huh? Were you saving the best for last?" Vivian smiles and winks.

Vivian: "Julian, have you ever bit into a real Georgia peach before? And I'm not talking about the ones that you buy in a store."

Me: "No, I can't say that I have."

Vivian: "Trust me when I tell you, it'll be the juiciest thing you've ever tasted."

Vivian leaned over and gave Olivia and I both a nice, long, wet kiss. She then stood up, got out of the hot tub, and dried herself off. She poured herself a glass of champagne and lit up a smoke. Olivia and I had our hands all over each other and couldn't stop kissing. Vivian just watched us while she sipped her champagne and enjoyed her smoke. It was right around the time that Vivian finished her smoke that Olivia and I finally got out of the hot tub. We dried off and walked over to Vivian. She and Olivia started kissing, while Vivian was stroking my shaft. I was starting to get plenty hard by now. Olivia and I took turns kissing Vivian until she grabbed our hands and led us up the stairs into her bedroom. Best wedding gift, ever.

www.ingramcontent.com/pod-product-compliance
Lightning Source LLC
LaVergne TN
LVHW010613100826
845148LV00014B/2953

* 9 7 9 8 2 1 8 3 1 3 7 4 6 *